Of All the Girls

Michele Rivera

Published by Michele Rivera, 2017.

Of All the Girls

Michele L. Rivera

I was lying in wait for you
Without knowing who you are
Or if you would ever arrive
I have whispered wants to demons and angels alike
I have ached in the corners of dark rooms
Broken and lost, I have aimlessly wandered
A thousand songs of sorrow, I have desperately cried
For you
So tell me, where did you come from?
How is it that you found me here on time
To tame the beast inside of me
To offer me a taste of your divinity
In this space where I become sheltered by you,
The only place you want to be
And in this lyrical moment, we define for one another
What it means to not be alone
What it feels like to be home

Chapter One

"No! I'm not going!" Ashton crossed her arms over her chest and glared at her mother, who stood in front of her in the middle of their living room. "You can't make me go."

"Actually," Mrs. Daniels challenged her daughter. "I can."

Ashton's gray eyes narrowed. "*Actually*, Mother," she retorted, her tone full of defiance. "you can't. I'm eighteen. You no longer have control over me."

Mrs. Daniels took a deep breath. "Ashton Elizabeth, so long as you are living under *my* roof, you will do what *I* tell you to and don't you dare try to argue with me, missy, because this is a battle you won't win." Mrs. Daniels met her daughter's hard stare with one of her own. "Understood?"

"Ugh!" Ashton ran her hands through her long, dark brown hair, curled loosely at the ends and tossed her head back to emphasize her frustration. "Why, Mom? Why?" Finally, she looked at her mother. "I don't want to go. I don't want to see him."

Ashton's mother tipped her head to the side, frowning. "Sweetie, he's your father."

Ashton's eyes widened, expectantly. "So?"

"So," Mrs. Daniels began. "He misses you and your brother. It's been eleven years since he's seen you and Noah. You're his children."

"Ha!" Ashton scoffed. "If we're that important to him then why did he abandon us for his secretary and move all the way to freaking Boston and make a new family? Who the hell wants to live in Boston anyways? It's like zero degrees year 'round."

"That's the point, Ash, it's about family. Your dad wants you and your brother to be a part of his life and his life just happens to include a second family," Mrs. Daniels explained.

"Mom, he shouldn't even have a second family! It's as if his first family wasn't good enough. How do you not hate him?"

"Hating someone is not good for one's aura."

Ashton rolled her eyes. "Maaa!" She whined. "Please don't be weird."

"It's not weird. It's true," Mrs. Daniels said. "Hating someone takes a lot of energy from a person's spirit. That energy should be used to love other people." She sighed. "I never hated your father for what he did. He hurt us a great deal, but I used my energy to forgive him and to heal. Sweetie, you can't carry around this kind of resentment for the rest of your life. It's not worth your energy. Does that make sense?"

Ashton shrugged. "I guess, but I am *not* using my energy to love him. Nope."

"You don't have to love him, but you have to try to forgive him...for your own well-being. He's not a bad man, and if it weren't for him, I wouldn't have you and Noah and you two are the most wonderful things that could have ever happened to me."

"Sure we are," Ashton mumbled.

"Because we're awesome!" A baritone voice exclaimed from the sofa to the left of where Ashton and Mrs. Daniels stood.

Ashton turned to face her brother and glowered at him. "You, shut up. I don't even know how you're okay with any of this. Do you really want to spend the entire summer in Boston, away from our friends?"

"And get acquainted with some hotties from Massachusetts? Um, yeah, I want that." Noah's blue eyes lit up as a mischievous grin spread over his lips.

"Aargh! Seriously, dude! Are girls the only thing you think about?" Ashton asked him.

Noah snorted. "Says the lesbian."

Ashton held up her right hand, raising her index, middle and ring fingers at Noah. "Read between the lines, buddy. Read between the lines."

Mrs. Daniels cleared her throat, making her presence known. "Ashton, don't flip your brother off," she chided and then looked to her son. "Noah, don't tease your sister about her lesbianism."

"Sorry, Mom," Noah and Ashton grumbled in unison.

Noah stood up, his six foot stature towering four inches above Ashton. "Ash, look at it this way: we're getting a free vacation from Florida for three months. It'll be an adventure."

"Do you hear yourself?" Ashton asked her brother. "People don't leave Florida to vacation in Boston. That's against the natural order of things. It works the other way around. People from *Boston* come to *Florida* because Florida's better. Duh."

Noah laughed. "Not the part of Florida we're from. There's nothing here."

"I like it here," Ashton said. "It's peaceful."

"Sweetheart," Mrs. Daniels spoke in a gentle tone. "Listen to your brother. It's only for three months. It's your father's high school graduation gift to the both of you and you'll get meet his wife, her daughter—who I believe is about your age— and their newborn. Don't you want to meet the baby?"

Ashton raised a skeptical eyebrow at her mother. "Ma, just because I did a nannying gig once doesn't mean I want to fly all the way over to Boston to meet a baby."

"That baby is your half-sister," Mrs. Daniels said. "She's your family. Do I have to give you the family speech again?"

Noah put his hand on Ashton's shoulder. "Please don't make her give the speech again."

Ashton shook her head. "You're my twin, Noah. You should be on my side."

"Don't do that." Noah wagged his finger at Ashton. "Don't use the twin thing. You know I got your back. I think this trip could be good for us. Maybe it'll even be fun."

Ashton chewed the inside of her cheek and looked at her mother for several seconds in silence until finally she spoke, "Mom, what dad did to us was wrong."

Mrs. Daniels gave Ashton a small smile. "I know and he's trying to make amends. Give him a chance," she said. "If you made a poor decision, wouldn't you want the chance to be forgiven?"

Ashton glanced at her brother, the floor, and then at her mother. "Yes," she said, her voice barely audible.

Mrs. Daniels's smile widened. "Then it's a done deal! You're both spending this summer in Boston to reestablish a relationship with your father! How lovely!" She wrapped her arms around her children, pulling them into a tight embrace. "I'm gonna miss you two rascals." After she kissed the cheeks of both Noah and Ashton, Mrs. Daniels released them from her grip. "Now go pack."

Ashton gasped. "What? When do we have to leave by?"

"Saturday," Mrs. Daniels said.

"But today's Thursday," Ashton pointed out the obvious.

"Exactly," Mrs. Daniels said, smiling. "I had your father purchase the tickets for the soonest flight out knowing that when it comes down to it, I wasn't going to give either of you a choice in the matter except to go. Furthermore, I didn't want to give either of you any extra time to beg me to stay here. So you better get to packing. Chop chop."

***

Ashton grabbed a pair of skinny jeans from her dresser drawer, held them up to scrutinize them. She peered over at her best friend, Katlyn, who was sitting on the edge of Ashton's full-size bed, flipping through the latest edition of *Well-Read Lez* magazine.

"What about these?" Ashton asked her friend. "Should I bring them?"

Katlyn glanced up at Ashton. "Yes! Those make your ass look fantastic!"

Ashton pressed her lips together and forced a smile. "Thanks, Kat, but I'm not going to Boston to impress anyone."

Katlyn shrugged. "You never know. I heard there's a lot of gay girls in Boston. You could maybe find yourself a lady friend." She grinned. "A summer fling, if you will."

"I will not," Ashton said flatly. She folded the jeans and placed them in the open suitcase at the foot of the mattress. She tilted her head to the side thoughtfully and pouted at Katlyn. "So you don't think my other jeans make my ass look fantastic?"

Katlyn began laughing. "No, doofus, that's not what I meant. You rarely wear form-fitting clothes and you can actually make out your figure in that particular pair, which is a good thing because you have a great body...a runner's body."

Ashton rolled her eyes. "That's probably because I'm a runner." She put a few plain, black tank tops in the suitcase. "Ugh. That reminds me—I have to pack my sneakers." She groaned. "How am I supposed to cram everything I need into two suitcases? This sucks!"

"It sure as hell sucks. You're preaching to the choir," Katlyn said. "My bestie is ditching me for the whole summer!"

"Kat, I'm not ditching you. It isn't like that. I had no choice."

"I know, I know. Family blahbidy blah." Katlyn's shoulders sagged. "We'll still talk all the time though, right?"

"Of course!" Ashton reassured her friend. "And we can video chat on Instavisit."

Katlyn held out her pinky. "Promise?"

Ashton walked towards her friend and coiled her pinky around Katlyn's. "I pinky promise."

"Okay," Katlyn said with a nod. "Now as for your packing dilemma, you could always buy clothes while you're there. Boom. Problem solved. You're welcome."

"If I had money, yes, that would be a solution, but being a nanny hasn't exactly put me in the wealthy one percent of the population. You feel me?"

"Ash, your dad's a lawyer. I'm sure he has a credit card...or two to spare."

"I don't want his money, Kat. I don't want anything to do with him." Ashton's pitch rose slightly.

"Chill out, chica. I was just sayin'. There's no need to worry if you can't bring *everything* you own," Katlyn said. "There are loopholes. Square, plastic loopholes." She smirked, a devilish look in her light, brown eyes.

Ashton nodded. "Riiight." She smiled back at her friend. "You're bad."

"You love me."

"True story." Ashton put her hands on her hips and stared into her open closet. "How many sweatshirts do you think I should bring?"

"All of them. It's Boston. You've never left Florida. You're going up against some serious climate change, my friend. You could potentially freeze to death if you don't dress accordingly."

"I appreciate your optimism," Ashton said, straight-faced. "It's so very comforting."

"But of course." Katlyn closed the magazine in her hands and looked at Ashton, her mouth turned downwards. "But to be honest, it's really going to blow here without you. Who am I going to binge-watch *Folklore Legends* with?"

Ashton chuckled. "What about Matt?"

"Oh yeah, because a show about princes and princesses is right up my boyfriend's alley."

"Hmm." Ashton's eyebrows scrunched together as she ran her thumb over her chin. "What if you tell him it's soft porn?"

Katlyn grinned and aimed her forefinger at Ashton. "That could work. You're a genius."

"I have my moments." Ashton's gaze fell onto the bookshelf adjacent to the window in her room, where the last of the day's sunlight streamed through. "Shit."

"What?"

"My books, my e-reader, my mp3 player...I can't be without them," Ashton said solemnly.

"I'll give you the e-reader and the mp3 player, but books? Really? Why would you need books if you have your e-reader?"

"Because some of my favorite books aren't available for downloading and they're my..." Ashton trailed off and lowered her head.

"Your safety blanket," Katlyn supplied. "I get it."

"Then what do I do?"

"How about you pick your absolute fave and leave the other nine-hundred behind. They won't go anywhere while you're gone. Trust me."

Ashton let out a frustrated breath, trudged towards her collection of paperbacks and scanned the alphabetized titles. She gently removed a book from the shelf and pivoted on her heels to meet her friend's stare. She pressed the novel to her chest. "*Decoded Soul.* This is my pick."

"See? Crisis averted." Katlyn pointed to the suitcase. "Put it inside."

A sly grin suddenly replaced Ashton's previously saddened expression. "That's what she said."

Katlyn whooped. "Ha! You pervert."

"You love me." Ashton moved to the bed and deposited the book into her luggage.

"True story. Now explain to me again why you're opposed to dating while you're in Boston."

"Kat! Geez. Let it go." Ashton turned to face the mirror above her dresser. She took the black elastic band from her wrist and tied her wavy, dark chocolate mane back into a ponytail. She adjusted the straps of her camisole, straightened her shoulders, and whirled around to eye her friend. "Can you do that for me? Can you let it go?"

"Nah, I'd much rather nag you about it."

"Why is my love life so important to you?" Ashton inquired.

"Pfft. You mean your *lack* of a love life?"

"Whatever."

"Dude, this is your opportunity to hook up with all kinds of cuties for three months," Katlyn said. "This could be insanely good for you."

Ashton shot Katlyn a dubious glare. "Good for me how?"

"Ash, you've only ever been in a relationship. You need to spread your wings. Explore your options. Experience variety."

Ashton chuckled. "In other words, you think I should have copious amounts of sex with different women, yes?"

Katlyn's eyes grew wide with excitement. "Yeasss! Exactly!"

"Not my style."

"Aargh! Must you be this complicated?" Katlyn asked.

"There's nothing complicated about it. I'm a one woman kind of woman. It's actually quite simple." Ashton knit her brows together. "You're with Matt and *only* Matt. You're happy, aren't you?"

"For sure, I'm happy. But I've been with other boys before Matt, which is why I chose him because trial and error has shown me that he's the best. You, my dear, had one girlfriend for two years. That's it. Felicia is all you know." Katlyn sighed heavily. "I'm just saying that you should shop around a little before settling on your next bae. This way you can be more certain that whoever you end up with is the best person for you."

Ashton nodded slowly. "Alright. There are two things going on here that we need to address: one, never use the word 'bae' in my presence again." She gave Katlyn an unsparing stare. "Two, what is this really about?"

Katlyn worried her bottom lip. "I just don't want you to get yourself into any more...um... bad situations. You deserve someone who treats you—"

"Hey!" Ashton threw her palm up to silence her friend. "We agreed that we weren't going to talk about that. Ever."

"I know, but—"

"Ever!"

Katlyn exhaled. "Fine."

"Thank you."

"Let's pretend though that you happen upon someone in Boston who's mind-blowing," Katlyn proposed. "Would you at least consider dating them?"

"No."

"Why the fuck not?"

"Whoa." Ashton opened her arms. "Watch your fucking language." She gave Katlyn a playful look and the girls shared a brief laugh.

"Okay. All kidding aside, why wouldn't you date a mind-blowing Bostonese?" Katlyn asked.

Ashton giggled. "I think they're called 'Bostonians,' you goofball."

"Same diff." Katlyn stuck her tongue out at Ashton. "Now stop trying to distract me and answer my question."

"Ugh. If I answer, you're buying when we go to The Bean later," Ashton said.

"Done."

"I wouldn't get involved with anyone from Boston because eventually, I'd come back here and they'd still be there and then I'd end up in a long distance relationship, which isn't something I want. Satisfied?"

"Or you could hook up with them while you're there and then...unhook with them when you leave. Also known as *dating* instead of relationshipping." Katlyn smirked.

Ashton rolled her eyes. "Noted. May we please be finished with this conversation now?"

"We'll table it."

Chapter Two

Ashton knocked lightly on her brother's bedroom door, leaned her forehead against it, and gripped the doorknob. "Noah? Can I come in?"

"It's unlocked," he called back from inside the room.

Ashton turned the knob and opened the door. She stood in the entryway and leaned wearily to the left, her shoulder pressed into the wooden panel. She gave her brother's living quarters a once-over before her eyes landed on him. Noah was sitting cross-legged on the carpeted floor holding the controller to his video game console. He stared attentively at the screen in front of him as his thumbs moved quickly from button to button. A loud noise akin to an explosion blasted through the speakers. "Nooo!" Noah cried and dropped the controller. He craned his neck to look at Ashton. "I died," he said. "They blew me up."

"Zombies?" Ashton asked.

Noah shook his head. "Alien invasion."

Ashton nodded. "Sorry."

"It's alright. I'll get those bastards next time." He rose from the floor and combed his hands through his sandy blonde crew cut. "Are you just gonna creepily lurk in the doorway or do you want to come in?"

"I'll stay where I am. It smells like a locker room in here." Ashton scrunched up her nose.

"Does not."

"Dude, yes it does. It's an extremely unpleasant mixture of sweat and pricey cologne. Eww."

Noah shrugged. "Suit yourself, little miss fancy pants."

"Screw you, butthole."

"Wow." Noah sniggered. "Someone's bad moody."

"Am not."

"Ash, don't even try lying. What's wrong? Level with me."

"I'm tired and I can't sleep," Ashton grumbled. "How is it Friday night already?"

"Ah." Noah nodded. "I get it. This is about tomorrow, isn't it?"

Ashton straightened her stance, eyes wide. "Well, duh! Of course this is about tomorrow. I don't want to go. I don't want to leave Florida."

"Really?" Noah asked in mocking tone. "I would have never known since you only mentioned it seven thousand times."

"Ugh. I'm serious, man."

"Yeah. I get that," Noah said. "But it's happening. We're getting on that plane to Boston in the morning. You just have to accept it or you're going to be miserable for the next three months."

"I'm going to be miserable for the next three months anyways."

"I don't know what to tell you," Noah said.

"What if *you* go and represent the both of us?" Ashton suggested. "As twins, we're basically the same person."

"That's false and you know it. Therefore, I feel confident in saying that I don't think that's a viable option."

Ashton muttered several obscenities under her breath then sighed dramatically. "How are you so cool about this? Our lives are being uprooted despite our opposition and you're going along with it all calm and...stuff."

"Because I've come to the conclusion that there's no use in being upset over something we can't change, and we can't change this, Ash." Noah spoke in a low tone. "You might as well make it easier on yourself and follow my lead."

Ashton gave her brother a defeated look. "Do you whole-heartedly believe that if I accept our circumstances, it won't be as bad?"

"I do," Noah said firmly. "This could turn out to be the best summer ever."

Ashton raised an eyebrow at Noah. "I doubt that."

"You never know. Anything's possible."

***

Ashton and Noah huddled together by the automatic exit doors of the Boston International Airport. Four large suitcases and two backpacks encircled them.

Ashton glanced down at their luggage.

"Do you think this will all fit in his car?" She asked Noah.

Noah's shoulders rose slightly. "It should be fine."

"What if it's not fine, though?"

"Then we'll figure it out," Noah said.

Ashton scoured her surroundings. "This place is dingy," she remarked. "And it's poorly lit. The airport in Florida where we caught our flight was way nicer."

Noah rubbed the back of his neck. "Are you through complaining?"

"Not even close." Ashton motioned with her head to the food vendor stationed across from them. "What the hell is Dippin' Dough?"

Noah studied the food stand for a moment. "It appears to be a coffee and doughnut shop."

Ashton scoffed. "Why would anyone name a coffee place Dippin' Dough? That makes no sense. Like none."

"Maybe it's a Boston thing."

"Oh nooo," Ashton gasped.

"What now?"

Ashton looked gravely at her brother. "What if they don't have The Bean here?"

"Jesus, Ash. Could you be more theatrical?"

"Is that a rhetorical question?" Ashton replied. "Because if not, then yes. I can absolutely be more theatrical."

"Please don't be. You're annoying enough already."

"Psht. You're annoying."

Noah rolled his eyes and Ashton jabbed him in the shoulder with her fist. "Dude, this is a real concern of mine," she said. "If there is no Bean, how will I fuel my caffeine addiction?"

"You can find a new dealer." Noah aimed his index finger straight ahead. "There. You can try Dippin' Dough."

"Not happening."

"Then you can brew coffee at home," Noah offered. "I'm sure dad has a coffee maker."

Ashton's eyes grew dark and wide. "Whoa. No. No. Don't say that. This is not home. Our home is in Florida...with mom. This is our temporary residence." She paused for effect. "And can we really rely on our father to have a coffee maker? We can't even rely on him to pick us up at the airport on time."

Noah glimpsed at the watch on his left wrist. "We landed almost forty-five minutes early, which he probably didn't expect. Give him a break. Mom said he'll be here at one o'clock so let's just *patiently* wait for him for another fifteen minutes."

Ashton gaped.

"Ugh. Why are you giving me your death stare?" Noah asked Ashton.

"Because once again, you're not siding with me. I'm your sister. We shared a womb, Noah. A freaking womb. He's practically a stranger. You're supposed have *my* back."

"I do have your back."

"Riiight." Ashton's voice oozed with sarcasm. She reached into the front pocket of her boot cut jeans and retrieved her cell phone. "I'm going to call mom to tell her we arrived safely."

"Way to avoid conflict by changing topics. Brava."

"I have no idea what you're talking about," Ashton said nonchalantly as she hit a button on the phone and placed it up to her ear. After only a single ring, there was answer on the other end of the line.

"Sweetie?" Mrs. Daniels said.

"Hey, Mom. I wanted you to know that Noah and I landed safely."

"Oh good. How was the flight?"

Ashton tapped the tip of her right sneaker repeatedly against one of the suitcases. "The flight was...okay, I guess. I slept the whole time."

"You slept through your very first experience flying?" her mother asked.

"Yeah. I might have taken a sedative before we boarded the plane."

"Why?"

"Because I wanted to sleep, Ma," Ashton said.

"And your brother?"

"He watched a movie on his tablet."

Mrs. Daniels sighed disappointedly. “Well, you’re both safe. That’s what matters. Is your father there yet?”

“Nope. We arrived earlier than we were scheduled to.”

“I’m sure he’ll be there soon.”

“Yay,” Ashton muttered.

“Try to have an open mind about this. Please.”

“You bet.”

“How’s the weather?” Mrs. Daniels asked.

“The weather app on my phone says it’s sixty-five degrees but we’re still inside the airport.” Ashton kicked the suitcase with a little more force. “Mom, we came *from* a warm, seventy-three degrees in the early *morning* TO a nippy, sixty-five degrees in the *afternoon*. It’s June! That’s ludicrous!”

“You’re on the East Coast now. If you’re cold, put on a sweatshirt. After a while, you’ll adapt.”

“Thanks for your empathy, Mom.”

“You’re welcome. May I talk to Noah?”

“Be my guest.”

“I love you,” Mrs. Daniels said.

“Love you.” Ashton passed the phone to Noah. “Mom’s asking for you.”

Noah took the phone from Ashton, spoke several, incoherent, one-syllable words into the receiver, ended the call and handed the cellular back to his sister. Ashton stared at Noah, her mouth agape as she took the phone from him.

“Jeez, aren’t you ever the chatty fella today,” Ashton wisecracked. “What’s your trick to keeping convos with mom so short?”

“I don’t bitch about everything.”

“Rude!”

“It’s not rude, it’s true,” Noah said.

“It isn’t bitching, it’s me expressing my feelings.”

“Uh. No. It’s you bi—”

“Noah? Ashton?” an unfamiliar, bassy voice asked.

Ashton and Noah turned their attention at the same time to the older gentleman standing before them. He was slightly taller than Noah with similar blue eyes. He had a short buzz cut but the color of his hair was clearly a deep shade of brown, resembling Ashton’s. The three of them were unmistakably related.

“Yeah?” Noah answered.

He gave them a warm smile. "It's me!" He opened his arms and approached them for a hug. "It's Dad!"

Ashton took a step back, closer to her brother. Noah stuck his hand out for the man to shake. "Hi."

Mr. Daniels cleared his throat, his arms falling quickly to his sides for a second. He nodded, forcing his smile to remain intact. Then he reached out with his left hand to greet Noah. "Hi, son," he said as they shook hands. After their brief salutation was over, Mr. Daniels faced Ashton and offered her the same hand he had shaken Noah's with. "Hello, Ashton."

Ashton clutched tightly to the handle of the suitcase in front of her. She glanced at her father's out-stretched hand then stared at him. "Hello, Dean." Her tone was indifferent. Mr. Daniels nodded again and pulled his arm away. He tipped his head to the side a bit as his eyes danced between his children in silence. Then he furnished another smile, nearly beaming.

"God, it's good to see you two! You're all grown up and...grown up. You look great! Even better than the pictures your mother's sent me." He clapped his hands together. "I'm so glad you're here. Thank you both for coming. It means more to me than you know."

"Swell," Ashton mumbled. "Now that we're all reunited and such, can we please leave the airport?" she asked her father.

Mr. Daniels chuckled. "We sure can! How was the flight?"

"Fine," Ashton and Noah said in concert.

"Are you guys hungry?" Mr. Daniels asked. "You must be hungry. I took the liberty of making lunch reservations for us at one of Boston's best Italian restaurants." He lifted Ashton's knapsack from the floor and slung it over his shoulder. "Your step-mother...um...Regina and her daughter, Chloe will be meeting us there. Then when we get back to the house, I'll introduce you to Ariel."

"Who's Ariel?" Ashton asked.

Mr. Daniels grinned. "Why she's your baby sister! She's at home with the nanny."

Ashton raised her eyebrows. "You named your daughter after a fictional mermaid? That's rich."

"A foxy mermaid," Noah added.

Ashton whacked Noah upside his head. "Don't be gross."

"I'm not being gross. I'm stating the facts," Noah said.

"I chose that name because growing up, Ariel was your favorite character in *The Mermaid that Could*," Mr. Daniels said to Ashton. "Remember?"

Ashton inhaled. "I remember," she said quietly. "That's only because the other mermaids in the kingdom were pricks."

"And because you had a crush on her," Noah said.

Ashton whacked Noah again.

"Ouch! Stop hitting me!" Noah gave Ashton a slight push.

"Then stop saying dumb shit. I did not have a crush on her. She's a cartoon."

"You were a little obsessed," Mr. Daniels said. His comment was followed by the sound of Noah's laughter.

"Aargh! I'm so done with you both." Ashton grabbed the handles of her two large suitcases and started for the exit, wheeling her luggage behind her. "Are you coming or what?" she called out to Noah and her father. "Jerks."

Chapter Three

"Welcome to Elise's Italian Cuisine," Mr. Daniels said as he held the restaurant's door open for Ashton and Noah to pass through. Once the three of them were inside, Ashton surveyed her surroundings. The establishment was small and quaint. The lighting was dim even though it was still afternoon. There were only five booths lining the back end of the restaurant, six large tables in the main dining area, and one table for two by a large portrait of a bottle wine hung from the wall to their left.

"There she is." Mr. Daniels pointed to one of the booths, where a woman sat, waving at them. "Come on," he urged Ashton and Noah, who dutifully tailed him except that each of Ashton's steps were made with reluctance.

When they reached the table, the woman got up from her seat. She was of average height and wore her hair in a short, black pixie cut. Her eyes were light brown appeared to be kind, but Ashton remained wary.

Mr. Daniels leaned over and kissed the woman on her cheek. "Hi, honey," he said softly to her before straightening up. He placed his hand on Noah's bicep. "Noah, Ashton, this is my wife, Regina." He glanced tentatively at his children. "Regina, meet Noah and Ashton."

Regina did not attempt to shake either Ashton's or Noah's hands. She merely gave them both a friendly nod of acknowledgement.

A brief, awkward silence surrounded their party of four before Mr. Daniels spoke to dispel it. "Shall we all sit?"

Ashton sat beside Noah on one bench while Mr. Daniels and Regina took their seats across from them.

"Chloe should be here any minute," Regina said, addressing the group. "I apologize for her tardiness."

"Hun, it's alright," Mr. Daniels assured Regina.

Ashton sighed, rested her arms on the table, and opened the menu in front of her though she had no appetite. She leafed through the pages, feigning interest in her options. She glanced up at her brother, who was carefully viewing each item listed. With a slight shake of her head, Ashton's gaze veered to the cloth napkin beneath her right wrist. She pinched the folded edges of its material between her forefinger and thumb.

"You okay, Ash?" Noah asked.

Ashton's eyes returned to Noah. "Huh? Oh. Yeah. I'm fine."

Mr. Daniels looked at Ashton. "Do you know what you're going to order?"

She faced her father. "I'm still deciding." She smiled weakly at him when the chimes above the restaurant's entrance door jangled, deflecting Ashton's focus to the direction of the noise. Her sights immediately fell on the young woman stepping into Elise's Italian Cuisine. Ashton's jaw slackened slightly, her gaze fixed on the tall, blonde figure sporting dark wash jeggings, brown leather boots laced up to the middle of her calves, and a white, deep v-neck t-shirt. A long, silver pendant hung low between her medium-sized bust. Ashton swallowed, her eyes moving upwards to the young woman's face again. Her skin was fair, her lips were a vibrant shade of red, and her hair was a wavy, golden bob that fell to her shoulders with layered ends and side-swept bangs. She was breathtaking, and without warning, she turned towards Ashton and began striding down a path to the booth where Ashton, Noah, Mr. Daniels, and Regina were sitting.

The young woman waved at the four of them. "Mom! Dean!"

Regina looked to the source of the voice and smiled broadly. "Chloe!"

Ashton's heart dropped to the floor of her stomach. *That's Chloe?*

"*That's* Chloe?" Noah whispered to Ashton.

"Shh!" Ashton hissed and quickly resumed skimming the menu.

Mr. Daniels stood up. "Chloe, hi. Thank you for joining us," he said. "This is my son, Noah, and my daughter, Ashton." He pointed at them as he spoke their names.

Noah rose from the bench and shook Chloe's hand. "Hi. It's so great to finally meet you."

"Same," Chloe replied.

As Noah returned to his seat, Ashton glimpsed at Chloe, who was already regarding her. Ashton shifted uncomfortably and the corners of Chloe's mouth curled into what almost appeared to be a smirk.

"Hey," Chloe said to Ashton.

Ashton lifted her arm from the table in a mock wave, but remained silent.

"Why don't you sit next to your mother," Mr. Daniels suggested to Chloe. Regina nodded in agreement and slid off the bench. Chloe slipped into the middle of the booth beside Mr. Daniels and Regina sat back down.

"You're late," Regina spoke under her breath to Chloe.

"Sorry. My date with Trevor went into overtime," Chloe said in a tone as low as her mother's.

"Mind your manners, young lady," Regina murmured.

"Yes, Mother." Chloe then directed her blackish-brown eyes at Ashton, whose astounded stare had never completely left her. Chloe arched an inquisitive brow at Ashton, who immediately became overly concerned with her glass of water. "So you two are from the Sunshine State, huh?" Chloe asked Ashton and Noah.

"That's right," Noah said.

"Must be nice there with all the Palm Trees and beautiful beaches."

"It is," Noah confirmed.

"Are you guys jonesing to get outta here yet?" Chloe asked.

"Chloe, stop," Regina rebuked. "They just arrived not two hours ago."

"Yes," Ashton said softly.

Chloe bit her painted bottom lip and smiled crookedly at Ashton. "She *can* speak."

An unforgiving blush burned Ashton's cheeks.

"Excuse me?" Regina asked Ashton.

"Yes," Ashton reiterated. "I want to go home...to Florida."

"Alright. That's enough," Mr. Daniels said sternly. "Chloe, please be more punctual in the future and Ashton, you're here in Boston. You need to come to terms with that." He took a sip of his gin and tonic.

"Way to go," Noah mumbled to Ashton.

"Bite me," Ashton spoke under her breath to her brother.

"I was thinking," Mr. Daniels began, "Chloe, why don't take Noah and Ashton out tonight to wherever is hip? Show them around. Get them acquainted with the city and you three can get acquainted with each other."

"What?" Chloe and Ashton gasped at once.

"Is there a problem?" Mr. Daniels asked the girls.

"Um. It's...it's Saturday night," Chloe said. "I have plans already."

"Then change them to accommodate our guests," Regina said to Chloe.

"No," Ashton said in haste. "It's cool because I have to...er...unpack."

"Ash, you have all summer to unpack," Mr. Daniels said.

Noah chuckled. "I, for one, think it's a totally bril idea, Dad."

Ashton knocked her knee into Noah's leg under the table. "I thought you were gonna help me," she said to her brother.

Noah shrugged. "You thought wrong."

"Chloe, what do you have planned?" Regina asked.

Chloe began rapping her fork against her placemat. "I was going to hit up that club I told you about, Mercury."

"Excellent!" Regina grinned. "Ashton and Noah will accompany you."

Chloe turned to her mother. "They will?"

Ashton frowned at her father. "We will?"

"A club? In the city?" Noah rubbed his hands together enthusiastically. "Yeah, we will!"

Chapter Four

Ashton perched her tablet atop the dresser in what was to be her bedroom for the following three months. She sat at the foot of the bed and stared at Katlyn's face on the tablet's screen.

"I could hitch a ride back to Florida," Ashton said.

"Oh, that's safe." Katlyn rolled her eyes. "Dude, you've seen as many episodes of *Psychotic Intellect* as I have. Hitchhiking is a surefire way to be murdered. Do you want to be murdered? Do you?"

Ashton exhaled and shook her head. "No."

"No. You don't. Exactly. Now tell me more about your day so far. Was it weird reuniting with your dad?"

"You mean, *Dean*?" Ashton corrected.

"You call your dad by his first name?"

"You bet I do."

"That's a teensy bit harsh," Katlyn said.

"Pshh. It's way less harsh than bastard."

"Point taken." Katlyn nodded as she spoke. "How's step-Madre?"

"Regina?"

"Yeah. Her."

"Kat, she's the woman my father left my mother for. Do you really think I have anything favorable to say about her?"

"Well, have you gotten to know her?"

"No, but you're hilarious for thinking I would want to," Ashton said.

"Maybe you should. Maybe she's nice."

"I don't give a flying fuck if she's nice. Did you not hear the part about her once being my father's mistress?"

"Alright. Chillax, Ash. I'm aborting the topic."

"Thank you."

"How's the baby?" Katlyn asked. "Is she precious?"

Ashton smiled a little. "She is." Her expression immediately sobered. "You know, considering whom she's the spawn of."

"Quit being such an asswipe!" Katlyn demanded.

Ashton gave Katlyn the middle finger.

Katlyn drew in a sharp intake of air. "Now, now, we both know you don't mean that." She grinned. "But here's an idea: why don't you go find yourself a hot, city girl to finger."

Ashton's jaw fell open and Katlyn started laughing hysterically.

"You filthy fiend," Ashton said through a giggle of her own.

Within a few seconds, the girls caught their breath. Katlyn dabbed under her eyes with a tissue. "Okay, but in all seriousness, what's her name?"

"Whose name?"

"Your baby sister's, dummy."

"Ariel."

Katlyn squinted. "As in the merm—"

"Precisely."

"Awe. That's kinda sweet." Katlyn leaned forward in her chair and lowered her voice. "What's the deal with the older half-sister? Is she cool?"

"Whoa! Hold up! Chloe is NOT my half-sister. We don't share any DNA whatsoever. We are one hundred percent unrelated."

"My gods! No need to get your panties in a bunch," Katlyn said. "She's not related to you. Got it."

"Good."

"So is she cool? This Chloe chick?"

An unexpected rush of heat overcame Ashton, who promptly diverted her gaze from Katlyn to the carpet. "She's...um...she's whatever."

"Ash, what was that?"

"Heh? What was what?" Ashton asked without looking at her friend.

"You're blushing! Why are you blushing?"

"I'm not blushing."

"Are too," Katlyn said. "Spill! Why are blu–holy shit!"

"Whaaat?"

"Pretty girls always make you blush."

"Nuh-uh."

"Liarpants! They totes do!" Katlyn exclaimed.

"Where are you going with this?"

"She's a knockout isn't she? Chloe's a knockout and you're attracted to her...aren't you?!"

Ashton buried her face in both her palms and groaned.

"Dude, you *have* to tell me," Katlyn implored. "I won't judge you. This is a judgment-free space."

Ashton uncovered her face and stared at the tablet. Her eyes bore into the screen. "No! I am in no way attracted to her."

Katlyn nodded. "Fine, but on a scale of one to ten, what would you rate her?"

"Kat! I'm not going to rate her." Ashton shook her head. "She's a looker. I'll say that much. Alright?"

Katlyn grinned and opened her mouth to speak, but was cut off by a voice in the distance.

"You think I'm a looker, huh?" Chloe stood in the doorway of Ashton's room, arms folded across her chest.

"Oh boy," Katlyn whispered as Ashton jumped up from where she had been sitting on the bed. With her right hand over her heart and all the color gone from her complexion, Ashton spun around to confront Chloe.

"I...er...that's not..." Ashton pointed to the tablet on top of the dresser. "I was...and yeah."

"It's fine," Chloe said.

"But...but that's not..." Ashton exhaled and blinked deliberately. "I'm sorry."

Chloe shrugged. "Don't be. I'm flattered." She smirked at Ashton. "You're not so bad yourself."

"Um...thanks?"

Chloe motioned to the bedroom door with her head. "For future reference, there's a lock on this thing. You might want to use it."

A muffled laugh came from Katlyn's end of the tablet.

"I will surely do that," Ashton said to Chloe.

"I was sent up here by your father to see if you were almost ready," Chloe explained. "It's half past eight. We're heading out to the club soon."

"I'll be down in a sec."

"Okey-doke." Chloe grabbed ahold of the doorknob and shut the door behind her as she exited the room.

"Wow. That sucked," Katlyn said. "And I can't believe you failed to mention that you're going clubbing tonight!"

Ashton glared at her friend. "Don't."

Chapter Five

Chloe rounded the tan SUV parked in the driveway of her home, opened the door to the driver's side, and got in.

"I call shotgun!" Noah hollered and hopped in the passenger's seat of the vehicle.

"You're such a goober," Ashton said to Noah as she climbed into the backseat behind Noah, which provided her with a decent view of the right side of Chloe's profile.

Chloe exhaled loudly and swerved in her seat to face Noah and Ashton. "Look, you guys, please don't embarrass me tonight."

Ashton scoffed. "You think we're an embarrassment? Seriously?"

Chloe shook her head. "That's not what I said."

"How would we embarrass you?" Noah asked.

"By using words like 'goober' in public," Chloe answered.

Ashton gripped the headrest of Noah's seat. "I'll have you know that 'goober' is a perfectly appropriate vocabulary word that's just way underappreciated and therefore it's hardly used."

"No." Chloe repositioned herself, turning forward in her seat and started the engine. "It's hardly used because it's purposeless."

"Are you always this snooty?" Ashton asked Chloe.

"I am not snooty." Chloe's voice took on a defensive tone. "Are you always this sensitive?"

"Yes, she is," Noah said.

Ashton flicked the back of Noah's head. "The hell, dude?"

"Oww!" Noah smoothed his left hand over the sore spot of his skull. "You big meanie!"

"Aargh!" Chloe grabbed the steering wheel tightly with both hand. "This is the kind of shit I'm talking about with you two being embarrassing. Like, can you maybe cool it with the childish bickering?"

Ashton's eyes widened. "Oh so not only are we an embarrassment but we're also childish?"

"Ashton, for the love of Christ, will you stop manipulating my words," Chloe said.

Ashton's belly fluttered at the sound of her name being spoken by Chloe. *Get ahold of yourself, Ashton.* "That's not what I was doing."

"That is most definitely what you were doing."

"Ladies, ladies," Noah interjected. "Let's be rational about this. We're all eighteen so let's act our ages and handle this like the adults that we are."

"I'm actually nineteen." Chloe sighed. "But you make a valid case."

"Alright." Noah nodded. "Then we'll call a truce and carry on with our night."

"Truce," Ashton mumbled, glowering at Chloe.

"Truce." Chloe adjusted the rearview mirror and glanced back at Ashton. Their stares locked. "By the by, your sincerity is overwhelming." She stuck her tongue out at Ashton through a grin, fixed her eyes to the street ahead, lifted her foot from the brake pedal and began to drive.

Free from an audience, Ashton stuck her tongue out at Chloe in retaliation.

"I can see you in the mirror," Chloe said to Ashton.

A stain of crimson spread across Ashton's countenance. She instantly turned her head to look out the window. "Fuck my life," she mouthed to herself. "Why are you watching me anyhow?" Ashton asked Chloe.

"Because of what we agreed on earlier."

"Which was what?" Ashton pressed.

"That we each think that the other is a looker." Chloe chuckled, but kept her stare on the road.

Ashton's face grew even hotter.

"I'm sorry but what did you two agree on?" Noah asked Ashton and Chloe.

"Nothing," Ashton and Chloe replied simultaneously.

"Nothing," Ashton repeated for accentuation. Then she leaned her forehead against the window pane, shut her eyes, and silently prayed for the world to end.

***

Entering through the door of Mercury was like entering another realm of reality. A large man in a suit with a completely shaved head, who clearly spent one too many hours lifting weights at the gym stood in front of a yellow rope, checking everyone's ID since no persons under the age of eighteen were allowed admission. After careful inspection of Chloe, Ashton, and Noah's licenses, the man lifted the rope, permitting the three of them full access into the club.

If not for the flickering, fluorescent lights, which changed colors to the beat of deafening electronica music roaring through multiple colossal speakers, the establishment would have been entirely dark. Chloe led the way confidently past the mass of bodies in motion on the dance floor. With far less self-assurance, Ashton trailed her, clutching the forearm of an awestruck Noah at her side.

When they reached the bar, Chloe came to a halt and glanced behind her at Ashton and Noah. "You guys want something to drink? Water? Soda?" She pulled a credit card from the back pocket of her low-rise jeggings. Automatically, Ashton's eyes followed Chloe's hand and she took in Chloe's shapely thighs. Her breath momentarily caught in her throat.

"Ash? Hello?" Noah's voice tore Ashton from the trance she was in.

Ashton shook her head and looked up at her brother. "What?"

"Do you want a bevvie?" Noah asked. "We're getting Shirley Temples." His index finger wagged back and forth between himself and Chloe.

"Dean's picking up the tab," Chloe informed, but Ashton kept her eyes on Noah.

"I'll just have water, thanks," Ashton said.

Noah patted Ashton's back. "You okay? You totally zoned out."

Ashton nodded. "Yeah. I—"

"She was distracted," Chloe interjected.

Mortified, Ashton shot Chloe a look of dismay, her mouth slightly ajar.

Chloe shrugged. "You lack subtlety." She winked at Ashton then turned her attention to the bartender.

Ashton quickly glanced at Noah, who much to her relief, was too preoccupied ogling a crowd of minimally dressed girls on the dance floor to have noticed her and Chloe's interaction.

“Drinks!” Chloe shouted over the music, passing Noah a clear, plastic cup filled with reddish liquid and a bottle of water to Ashton. Noah took his beverage and raised it as if making a toast before taking a sip. Ashton timidly wrapped her fingers around the bottle being offered to her.

Chloe arched an eyebrow at Ashton. “It’s not gonna bite you.”

Ashton manufactured a smile. “I know. Thank you.”

Chloe smiled back. “You’re very welcome.” She leaned in closer to Ashton. Close enough so that Ashton got a whiff of her fruity, floral perfume. Ashton’s heart temporarily stopped and then started beating again with a violent slam against her chest. “Not that you’re not biteable though,” Chloe whispered into Ashton’s hair from behind.

Ashton froze and strained to keep her stare straight ahead at everyone on the dance floor, pretending to be unfazed by Chloe.

Noah gave his drink to Ashton. “Hold this for me, will ya? I’m going to get my groove on!” He grinned and before Ashton could protest, Noah was on his way to the center of the club.

“Sure. No problem, bro,” Ashton mumbled to herself.

“If you want to go dance, you can put the drinks on the bar,” Chloe said. “I’ll watch them.”

Ashton exhaled and found the gumption to turn and face Chloe. “I’ve got it under control.”

“You don’t like to dance?” Chloe sized up Ashton. “You look limber enough to be the dancing type.”

“Why do you keep doing that?”

Chloe bestowed Ashton with a seductive, half-smiled and narrowed her eyes. “What is it that you think I’m doing?”

Though the drinks in her possession were cold, Ashton’s palms began to clam up. “You’re trying to provoke me.”

“Gasp.” Chloe tipped her head to the side. “That’s a mighty serious accusation,” she said. “Is that really what you think I’m doing?”

“Yes it is.”

Chloe pursed her lips and nodded slowly. “Did it ever occur to you that I might actually be flirting with you?”

Ashton’s mouth went completely dry. She crinkled her face up and shook her head. “No,” she answered softly.

"Well, that's what I'm doing."

"Why?" Ashton managed.

"Why not?"

"Because it's...it's weird."

"How so?" Chloe took a seat at the bar and patted the stool beside her, gesturing for Ashton to join her. "Enlighten me."

"Do you really need me to spell it out for you?!" Ashton shouted angrily above the blaring music.

"I do! Please!"

Ashton rolled her eyes and hesitantly stepped towards the stool. She placed her water and Noah's Shirley Temple on the counter and sat down. She rubbed her moist palms over her denim-clad legs and held onto her knees. When Chloe's hand rested upon Ashton's shoulder, every muscle in Ashton's body tightened. Sensing Ashton's sudden rigidity, Chloe immediately removed her hand.

"Sorry," Chloe said, her voice laden with sincerity.

Ashton braced herself and turned to Chloe, whose ebony irises were staring at her, full of remorse. Despite herself, Ashton was at once transfixed by the blackness of Chloe's eyes. All of her indignation dissolved. "It's okay."

"Are we good?" Chloe asked.

"Define 'good,'" Ashton retorted.

Chloe smiled. "I'll take that as a 'yes.'" She sipped from her plastic cup then set it on the counter, her gaze locked on Ashton the whole time. "I'm waiting."

"For?"

"Um...your explanation about why you think it's weird for me to flirt with you."

Ashton snorted. "There's like a plethora of reasons."

Chloe bit back a laugh. "A plethora, huh?"

"Don't laugh at me."

"Who's laughing?"

"*You*! You're about to," Ashton said. "I can tell."

"Ah, but *actively* laughing versus *almost* laughing are very dissimilar." Chloe smirked. "That said, I wasn't laughing at you. So carry on now with your explanation and your plethora."

Ashton glowered at Chloe.

"Whoa. If looks could kill..." Chloe left her sentence unfinished as her full lips formed an amused, but nonetheless dazzling smile.

Ashton's stomach somersaulted. She gripped the edge of the bar in an attempt to maintain her composure. "Anyways, it's weird because my father married your mom."

"And?" Chloe looked at Ashton expectantly.

"And..." Ashton blinked rapidly. "And that makes us part of the same family."

"Right, but we're not related."

"But same family."

"But not related, and therefore, totally kosher." Chloe toyed with the pendant hanging from her neck. "What else ya got?"

"You."

Chloe let out a short laugh. "Me! What about me?"

"Are you even...I mean...do you...what's your..." Ashton shook her head, internally cringing at the babbling mess she had become.

Chloe casually swung her right leg over her left, bent one arm on her knee and rested her chin in her palm. Her black-brown eyes flashed, smiling on their own, stealing the oxygen from Ashton's lungs. "Want some help?"

"With what?"

"You were floundering."

Ashton put her hand on her chest. "Psht. Was not."

"Were too." Chloe smirked. "Lucky for you, I'm fluent in gibberish. And no, I'm not gay."

"How did you know that that's what I was going to ask?"

"It was pretty clear where you going with that."

"Then what are you?" Ashton asked. Right away, she shut her eyes and winced. "I apologize. That was ignorant."

"Yes it was."

"I apologized."

"I heard you and I accept your apology," Chloe said. "To answer your question, I'm human."

Ashton sighed. "I know, but you said you were flirting with me and I'm a woman and you're a woman."

"We're both women? You don't say."

"Aargh! I just...if you're not gay—"

"Ashton?"

Ashton's heart leapt when Chloe spoke her name. "Yeah?"

"Why are you so interested in my sexual identity?"

Ashton cleared her throat. "I...uh...because." She nodded, satisfied with her own answer. "Because I am."

"Mmm. Because why though?" Chloe took another drink of her Shirley Temple. "Because you want to know how the girl you're checking out swings?" She bit down on the small, red straw sticking out of the cup and grinned mischievously.

Ashton gaped.

"I wasn't joshing you when I told you that you lack subtlety," Chloe said.

"Well, it's no news to you that I think you're good looking so yeah, maybe that's why I want to know. I'm curious."

"*How* good looking do you think I am?"

Ashton glared at Chloe. "Don't push it."

Chloe shrugged. "Can't blame a girl for trying." She uncrossed her legs. "I'm pansexual."

Ashton fought to keep her face expressionless. "Okay. Thanks for telling me."

Chloe raised an eyebrow at Ashton. "Is pansexuality a foreign concept to you?"

"Alright. Have at it."

"Have at what?"

"Make fun of me for my unworldliness," Ashton said.

"No." Chloe shook her head and set her cup back on the bar. She met Ashton's gaze. "I'm not going to make fun you, but I am going educate you."

"Educate me then."

"The best way to put it is like this: see, as a lesbian, you're attracted to—"

"Wait. You're assuming I'm a lesbian because I think you're good looking?"

Chloe chuckled. "Wrong. I don't think anything. I *know* you're a lesbian because your father told me."

"Thanks a bunch, Dean," Ashton grumbled under her breath.

"So as a lesbian, you're attracted to women, right?"

"Right."

"As a person who identifies as pansexual, I'm attracted to people on a...broader spectrum," Chloe said. "For me, who I'm drawn to is less about their gender identity or what's between their legs and more about who they are as an individual." She exhaled. "Understand?"

"I understand."

"Cool."

"Does your mom know?" Ashton asked.

"She sure does...and Dean knows too. I came out when I was fourteen as bisexual, but when I was about sixteen, I realized my sexual orientation was more fluid than I initially thought."

"Were you scared?"

Chloe nodded. "A little bit, but then I talked to the teacher who ran the GSA at my high school, and she taught me about pansexuality."

"Nice. Thanks for sharing all of that with me."

"No prob."

"My high school didn't have a gay/straight alliance," Ashton said.

"Really? That must've sucked."

"It did suck. I relied heavily on the internet and cable television."

The girls experienced a short laugh together before Chloe coughed and quickly stood up. "I'm gonna go dance. You good here?"

Ashton wrinkled her forehead. "Um. Yeah." She raised her water bottle. "All good."

"Sweet." Chloe turned away from Ashton and moved towards the dance floor. Chloe's scent lingered. Ashton inhaled slowly. Suddenly, her gut twisted when she felt the swarm of butterflies float throughout her entire body. "Nooo," she breathed.

***

"How's it going?" Noah asked Ashton breathlessly before taking his Shirley Temple off of the bar and guzzling it.

"Super," Ashton said dryly.

Noah plunked down on the seat next to Ashton. "Why aren't you dancing?"

"*Everyone* here is a stranger. Everyone. I'm not comfortable dancing amongst a room of total strangers. At least in the clubs back home, *some* of the faces are familiar. For all we know, these people could be psychopaths seeking their next victim and we'd be the perfect targets because we're not from here and locals can spot outsiders from miles away." She looked over at her brother, who was staring at her with his enlarged blue eyes, astounded.

"You have got to stop watching *Psychotic Intellect*. Stat," Noah said. "It is royally fucking with your head."

"On the contrary, it's making me a more vigilant citizen."

Noah scoffed. "You're vigilant enough as it is."

"Justifiably so."

"Ash, you can't let what that bitch did ruin your life. Not everyone is like her."

"Don't call her names. Please."

"Why not? It's warranted."

"Just don't," Ashton said. "Okay?"

"Fine."

"Thank you." Ashton turned her gaze to the dance floor and her heart fell to the pit of her stomach.

Chloe was sandwiched between a boy about Noah's height and a scantily clad girl with flaming red hair. Chloe's arms were above her head as her hips swung side to side, and her head bobbed along with the bass of the song playing.

Ashton clenched her jaw, unable to look away from Chloe's body; her balletic movements.

"Well, she's extremely sociable." Noah motioned to Chloe with his empty, plastic cup, looking in the same direction as Ashton.

"Yeah."

"Dude!" Noah slapped Ashton's arm with the back of this hand. "Are you cruising her?"

Ashton gave herself a mental shake and faced Noah. "What? Who?"

"Chloe, that's who."

"No!" Ashton responded flatout.

"But you think she's cute?"

"She's...visually agreeable."

Noah's eyebrows scrunched together. "The fuck? So in English, you do think she's cute?"

Ashton shrugged. "Do you?"

"I'm fairly certain that anyone who can see her thinks she's cute. Myself included, but I'm not appraising her...with my eyeballs."

"Neither am I."

Noah nodded lazily, squinting. "Sure you weren't."

"And if I were, would that be an issue?" Ashton asked, diffidently.

"Uh...Affirmative because it would kind of be incestuous."

"Not really. We have no genetic relation." Ashton's rationalization to Kat from earlier that same evening echoed in her head.

"Yeah but she's in our family...almost sister-ishly."

"I definitely don't see her as a sister," Ashton said. "I have difficulty seeing Dean as our father."

"Jesus." Noah curled his upper lip. "Are you interested in her? In a romantic way?"

"No! I'm only saying that, technically, she's not off limits because she's not a blood relative." The panic began building in Ashton's chest, making it hard to breathe. "I'm laying out the facts to make my point. That's all."

"Point taken, but still..." Noah shuddered. "Too close to home. Literally." He glimpsed over at Chloe on the dance floor then at Ashton. "Besides, she'd be off limits for you regardless because she's straight...isn't she?"

"Negative. She's pansexual."

Noah's expression contorted in confusion. "Meaning?"

"I'll tell you later."

Noah reached in the pocket of his cargo pants and pulled out his cell phone. "No way am I waiting on you to tell me. I'm going online to Quest this shit."

"Go for it."

After several minutes of staring at the screen of his phone, Noah looked at Ashton. "Huh."

"Yup. My thoughts exactly."

"Why weren't we taught about this sort of thing in school?"

"Mmm hmm. My thoughts exactly."

"Is our hometown really *that* non-progressive?" Noah shook his head.

"It seems that way, doesn't it." Ashton sighed heavily. "On the bright side—"

"Whoa, whoa, whoa. Hold up. *You* have a bright side?"

"Fuck you. You know I'm inherently an optimist."

"A cautious optimist."

Ashton flipped her middle finger up at her brother. "Still an optimist, wise guy."

"Alright. What's your bright side then?"

"That we learned something new," Ashton said.

Noah nodded. "Of course that's your bright side. You're like an information-aholic."

"That's not a real thing."

"I'll make it a real thing. Watch me." Noah grinned then his mouth slowly shaped into an O. "I got it!"

"You got what?"

"Chloe informed you of something new. She *is* something new."

"So?" Ashton began ripping the wrapper off of her water bottle to avoid Noah's eyes.

"You find Chloe intriguing, is that it?"

Ashton gave Noah a one-handed shove. "Dude, knock it off! I never said that."

Noah chuckled. "You never had to."

"Bite me."

"I'm right, aren't I?" Noah grimaced. "Just remember, Ash...close to home."

"One, you're incorrect." Ashton struggled to keep her tone emotionless. "Two, this isn't our home."

Chapter Six

At a quarter to midnight, Ashton, Noah and Chloe walked through the front door of the two-story American Colonial style house, where the three of them would be residing together for the next several months. As they all started for the staircase, Mr. Daniels emerged from the living room to their left, wearing a long, navy blue robe, holding a white, ceramic mug.

"Hey, kids." He smiled amicably at Ashton, Noah and Chloe. "You're fifteen minutes ahead of curfew. Did you have a good time?"

"I had a great time!" Noah grinned and held up his cell phone. "Four fine females gave me their numbers."

Mr. Daniels chuckled at his son then looked to Ashton and Chloe. "Girls?"

"It was chill," Chloe said.

Mr. Daniels nodded. "Good."

Chloe extended her right hand to Mr. Daniels, handing him his credit card. "Thanks."

Mr. Daniels took the card and put it in the large pocket of his robe. "You're welcome." He glanced at Ashton. "Ashton, you're awfully quiet. Did you have fun?"

"It was okay," Ashton offered with a listless shrug.

Mr. Daniels forced another smile. "Alright then." He raised his mug. "Anyone care to join me in the kitchen for some peppermint tea?"

"Nah," Chloe said while Ashton shook her head, passing on the invitation.

"Sure." Noah took a step towards his father.

Mr. Daniels beamed. "Great!"

Ashton glared at Noah, who mouthed "What?" at her. Ashton rolled her eyes. "I'm going to bed," she announced and began plodding up the staircase.

"Goodnight," Mr. Daniels called after Ashton.

"'Night." Ashton replied without looking back.

***

After trading in her jeans and fitted tee for sweatpants and a soft pink, ribbed tank top, Ashton pulled her long, wavy, dark brunette hair up into a messy bun. She plopped down on the queen size bed and grabbed her phone off of the small, wooden side table. She typed Katlyn a text message.

Back from the club. How was your night?

Within seconds, Katlyn's response appeared.

You must provide me with all the deets! My night was a drag. Matt passed out during Folklore Legends. Total boyfriend fail.

Ashton laughed to herself and replied.

I'm sorry, dude. That IS a bummer. There aren't really any details to give. Chloe and Noah danced. I stayed on drink patrol.

Moments later, an emoji of a sad face appeared on Ashton's cell screen followed by Katlyn's message.

I get that you're not psyched about being there, but you can't let that keep you from participating in YOUR LIFE! Don't be a downer the whole summer. You're in a new place, surrounded by all new things to experience and I need to live vicariously through you so swear to me you'll try to have some fun. Like even a smidgen. Swear?

"Aargh." Ashton pushed her head into the pillow behind her then answered Kat.

I swear.

Katlyn wrote back immediately.

Fabulous! Now tell me...did Chloe say anything else to you about you calling her a 'looker'?

Ashton winced at the memory.

She was sort of flirty with me at the club.

Katlyn's reaction came in at rapid speed.

Oh my god!! So she's gay?

Ashton read Kat's question twice before answering.

She said she's pansexual.

About a minute passed before the next message from Katlyn came in.

Sorry. I had to look that up on the internet...that's new for me. Why don't they teach us this shit in school? Fuck home ec.

Ashton chuckled.

Haha! Yeah, I agree. I didn't know about it either before she explained it. I was embarrassed by my own ignorance.

Ashton's phone lit up with Katlyn's response.

Don't be embarrassed. You can't know EVERYTHING. So...did you flirt back?

Ashton scoffed then glanced in the corner of her phone's screen to check the time: 12:37 a.m.

No and it's late. I should try to get some sleep.

Katlyn texted back right away.

Ugh! You're crushing my soul! If you think she's a 'looker' then you should get in on the flirting. You said yourself that you aren't really related or whatever, thus you could totally date her and it would be totally legal. Dude, you SWORE you'd LIVE a little.

Ashton inhaled deeply.

Live, yes. I never swore that I'd date though. I'll talk to you soon, but NOT about this. Goodnight, Kat.

Before Katlyn could write back, Ashton ended the messaging session and placed her phone on the side table. Sluggishly, she sat up, turned sideways and dangled her legs over the edge of the bed. She still had to brush her teeth. "I do live," she mumbled.

"Talk to yourself often?" Chloe's voice manifested from the entrance of the room.

Ashton's heartbeat came to a forcible standstill. Her merciless blush returned, setting her cheeks and ears ablaze. She closed her eyes, took in a breath, steeled herself and looked over at Chloe. Ashton's stomach did a cartwheel.

Chloe was leaning against the wall, arms crossed over her chest, and a roguish smirk on her lips. She hadn't changed her outfit from earlier yet. She was undeniably striking.

With great effort, Ashton swallowed the lump in her throat. "No," she finally answered.

Chloe nodded and tipped her head the slightest bit towards the door. "You keep forgetting that thing locks."

Ashton got up from the bed. "And you keep forgetting to knock."

Chloe's eyes flickered. "Touché."

"Can I help you with something?"

Chloe looked Ashton up and down, pursed her lips and shook her head. "Is that what you sleep in?"

Ashton, remembering how thin the fabric of her top was, quickly grabbed a throw pillow from the bed and hugged it close to herself. "Do you have no filter?"

Chloe frowned. "You didn't have to cover up on account of me." She grinned. "Seriously."

Ashton glared at Chloe. "You should leave."

Chloe used her left foot to push herself off the wall and took a step towards Ashton. "And if I don't?"

Ashton's pulse quickened and her body warmed throughout. "Please go."

"I'll tell you what. I'll go if you agree to let me buy you a coffee tomorrow."

Ashton furrowed her brow. "Why would I agree to that?"

"Because tonight obviously wasn't your idea of high jinks, and I told Dean I'd do my best to make sure you and Noah enjoyed yourselves, and I know your brother did, but I failed you. So I'm asking for a chance to make it up to you."

"Is this my father's genius idea? For a redo?" Ashton asked.

"Nope. This is my brainchild."

"You didn't fail at anything. I don't want to be here in Boston. Nothing is going to make me enjoy it."

"Is that a challenge?"

"No," Ashton huffed. "It's my reality."

"I see, but perhaps we could alter your reality to make it bearable for you to be here."

"Why are you doing this? Is it a pity thing? If that's what this is, no thanks. I don't need your pity."

Chloe nodded. "Good because this isn't about pity." She sighed. "We're stuck living together for the summer and I think it would best for both of us if we...bonded or something."

"You want to bond over coffee?"

"I do."

Ashton curled her upper lip. "I don't even like coffee." She lied.

"Hmph. I totally had you pegged as a coffee drinker." Chloe shrugged. "Then we'll bond over tea."

"I prefer coffee." Ashton spoke softly into the pillow she was squeezing.

Chloe chuckled, made a fist drew her right elbow back, victoriously. "Yesss! I knew it!"

Ashton resisted smiling. "Don't be cocky."

Chloe subdued her delight. "This is a cockless zone." She tucked her lips behind her teeth to hinder another laugh as Ashton almost gave in to her own amusement, but successfully masked it with a glower.

"Sorry," Chloe said. "I had to."

"Are you done?"

"I am."

"Okay. I'll have coffee with you but I refuse to go to Dippin' Dough."

"Yuck!" Chloe exclaimed. "I would never. That would be cruel," she said. "I was gonna take you to The Bean."

Ashton smiled. "The Bean?"

Chloe smiled back. "I take it you're pro-Bean."

"For sure."

"Awesomesauce." Chloe lifted her cell phone from her front pocket. "What's your number?"

Ashton's eyebrows narrowed. "Why do you need my number? Your room is right next door."

"But if I have your number, I can text you instead of just waltzing in here. I thought you'd be all for that. Unless of course you want me to come—"

"904-901-8783," Ashton blurted.

Chloe's fingers moved deftly over the keypad on her cell as she programmed Ashton's number into her contacts, grinning. She looked up at Ashton once she finished. "How's ten-thirty-ish tomorrow?"

"That works fine."

"Excellent. If by some chance, we don't cross paths, I'll shoot you a text."

Ashton gave Chloe a curt nod. "Right."

Chloe turned and started for the door, but paused before exiting. She glanced over at Ashton. "One more thing."

Ashton rolled her eyes. "Whaaaat?"

"You have a nice smile. You should show it off more." Chloe winked at Ashton and left, the click of the door sounded behind her.

Ashton sat down slowly on the bed and let out a long awaited exhale. Her phone buzzed against the table. "For fuck's sake, Kat," she mumbled, tossed the pillow she had been holding aside, and picked the phone up. Ashton's belly flopped as she read the screen of her phone.

Hey there. It's Chloe. Now you have my number. Easy peasy. Sweet dreams, pretty lady.

Ashton shook her head, but a small smile spread across her lips. *She thinks I'm pretty.* "No!" Ashton slapped herself on the cheek. "Snap out of it!" She laid down. "Sleep it off, Ash. Sleep it off."

Chapter Seven

Ashton stood in front the full length mirror attached the back of her private bathroom door. She turned to the side, examining her backside in the skinny jeans she was wearing. She frowned. She faced frontwards, untucked only one side of her plaid shirt and folded the sleeves of her top to right below elbows. She nodded. "Good enough." She glanced at her watch. It was a little past ten o' clock in the morning. She still had at least fifteen minutes to get ready before it was time to get coffee with Chloe. Her palms began to sweat at the thought. Ashton spun around to eye herself in the vanity mirror above the sink. After showering earlier, she let her hair air dry, applying only a dab of product to prevent frizz. Now, her long, sheeny locks hung stylishly over her shoulders. She opened the medicine cabinet and contemplated the small tube of lip gloss on the bottom shelf. *It's not a date,* she silently chastised herself, deciding to forego any cosmetics...even though her selection was limited being that lip gloss was the only makeup she owned. She puckered her lips and stared at them intently. They weren't chapped and had a natural, dark pink pigmentation, giving them an organic luster. She smiled, content with her appearance. Immediately, she mentally checked herself and glared into the mirror. Cold, gray eyes reflected back at her. "It's not a date. It's not a date. It's not a—"

"If you repeat it three times, do you vanish to a magical land?" Noah asked, leaning against the bathroom's doorframe, a sportive grin on his scruffy face.

Ashton's gaze deviated from the mirror and onto her brother. "For crying out loud! Is it customary to enter without knocking in this household?!"

"I *did* knock, but maybe you didn't hear me over earsplitting orchestral music." Noah rolled his eyes.

Ashton wheeled around to face her brother. "It's not orchestral, dipshit. It's dubstep violin."

"Like I care," Noah said. "You missed breakfast. Regina made pancakes."

"Like I care." Ashton did her best imitation of Noah.

"You're a mean older sister."

"Ha! I was born twelve minutes before you," Ashton said. "That hardly qualifies as being older than you." She pursed her lips in thought for a second. "And I'm not mean."

"I disagree."

"Congratulations."

Noah pouted. "Anyways, aren't you hungry?"

"No." Ashton half shrugged. "Anyways, you know I don't even like pancakes."

"There was coffee. You like coffee."

"That I do, but I happen to be going out to get my fix."

Noah quirked an eyebrow at his sister. "Really? I find that quite interesting."

"Why?"

"During breakfast, Chloe mentioned that she, too, was going out for coffee this morning, but she didn't get into specifics." Noah squinted. "However, I'm seeing a connection," he said. "Are you and Chloe going for coffee together?"

Ashton pushed passed Noah, stepping out of the bathroom and into the bedroom to evade his inquisitive stare. "Yes we are." She spoke while slinging her shoulder bag on.

Noah studied Ashton for a moment. "Why are you dressed up?

Ashton scoffed. "Dude, I'm wearing jeans and flannel...to properly represent the stereotypical lesbian. It's super casual."

"You are representing, no doubt, but those aren't just any jeans. Those are skinny jeans, and you only wear skinny jeans when you're trying to spruce up your attire, which you rarely do unless..." Noah gasped. "Is this a date?"

"What?" Ashton asked, incredulously. "No! Nope. Uh. Uh. No way." She shook her head. "Besides, she said at lunch yesterday that she's dating some guy named Trevor. She's off the market."

Noah tapped his index finger against his lips. "Alright. Buuut, if she were *on* the market, would you call this a date?"

"I absolutely would not." Ashton got down on one knee and double-knotted the laces of her right sneaker for no other reason than to avoid looking at Noah.

"Reason being that it's slightly morally skewed to go on a date with someone IN YOUR FAMILY, right?"

"Wrong. Reason being that I'm not keen on dating...not Chloe, not anyone."

"Well, if you want my two cents—"

"I don't."

Noah cleared his throat. "I think you should date. It would be good for you to get out there and meet new people, potential suitors and what have you, but you should also bear in mind that if you do date, there are like a catrillion women in Boston *outside* of this house."

"Noah, This isn't a date. I'm not dating. And we've been through this," Ashton rose to finally meet her brother's eyes. "Chloe's a part of our family but she's not related to us, so hypothetically speaking, if this were a date, it would be completely morally sound."

"Eh." Noah wrinkled his nose. "It's too bizarre to be morally sound."

"You're too bizarre to be morally sound."

"That was a terrible comeback."

"Shut up and go," Ashton ordered. "I have plans to finish getting ready for." She latched onto Noah's left arm and began hauling him out of her room. "Also, for the record, our family is exceedingly non-traditional. You really need to open your mind."

Noah stood beneath the threshold of Ashton's bedroom and gaped. "I have an open mind." He pointed to his head. "This mind is crazy open."

"Then open it more. Mkay? Awesome. Goodbye now." Ashton shut the door in Noah's face.

***

At 10:31 a.m. Ashton was standing outside of Chloe's bedroom. She wiped the moisture from her palms onto her jeans, made a loose fist with her right hand and went to knock on the door, but hesitated. When Ashton's arm was still mid-air, Chloe opened the door. Ashton's heart passed over a beat and she momentarily lost her breath. Chloe arched her eyebrows at Ashton's raised hand.

"I think it's safe to put that down now." Chloe smiled.

Ashton's face reddened as she immediately dropped her arm to her side. "I...uh...I was about to knock."

"I gathered as much," Chloe said. "I heard footsteps in the hall and sensed a presence at my door. Figured it was you since we have a date scheduled for approximately this time."

"A social engagement," Ashton amended.

"Come again?"

"You said, 'date.'" That's not what this is. This is a social engagement."

Chloe pressed her lips together to curb a laugh. "Same diff."

"No. There's a distinction between them."

"There is, is there?" Chloe nodded, her plump, red lips molding into a smirk. "Care to clarify?"

"They're just not the same thing."

Chloe chuckled. "Wow. That's a compelling argument especially coming from the daughter of a lawyer."

"He wasn't exactly around to teach me his ways," Ashton said matter-of-factly.

"Right. Touchy subject. Got it." Chloe opened the door to her room all the way. "Would you like to come in?"

Ashton glanced over Chloe's shoulder at the unmade bed, overflowing hamper by the casement window, and the dresser drawers with clothes hanging out of them. "Um."

"It's a mess. I realize this," Chloe admitted. "So do you want to come in or what?"

Ashton looked at Chloe, unaware that Chloe was staring at her and their gazes locked. Chloe's deep, brown eyes were penetrating. An electric current surged through Ashton. Flushed and overcome by a myriad of emotions, Ashton quickly turned away and motioned with her thumb to the staircase behind her. "Nah. We should get a move on."

"Okay then." Chloe drew her words out slowly. "Off we go."

***

Ashton and Chloe stood side by side in the long line at The Bean. While Chloe browsed the menu board, Ashton canvassed the environment. The café was much larger than the one she frequented in Florida. There was a stage to set up on the far right end of the coffeehouse, which was surrounded by at least twelve round tables. Each table appeared to be occupied by a diverse population of customers including two men in business suits, a woman pushing a baby stroller back and forth as she attempted to coax the toddler across from her to eat the slices of apple in front of him, and three teenage girls excitedly taking pictures of their drinks with their cell phones. In spite of herself, Ashton inhaled the sweet fragrance wafting from Chloe every chance she got, becoming more intoxicated with each intake of air.

"Do you know what you're getting?" Chloe's voice was so close that it tickled Ashton's ear when she spoke, causing goosebumps to cover Ashton's arms and the back of her neck. Ashton took a deep breath, trying to slow the pace of her pulse before she turned to answer Chloe, but Chloe's scent was inescapable, making it nearly impossible for Ashton to control her heart's rapid contractions. Ashton swallowed hard and shifted her stance to confront Chloe, whose face was all too close to Ashton's. Casually, Ashton shifted her body weight onto her right leg and drew her head back slightly in an effort to create some distance between them.

Chloe cast Ashton the side-eye. "What? Do I smell bad?"

"Huh? What?"

"You moved away from me."

Ashton's mouth went dry. "No, I didn't."

Chloe let out a short laugh. "You totally did."

"Okay, but only because you were up in my personal space."

"Suuure."

Ashton gaped. "You were."

"It wasn't because I make you nervous?" Chloe queried.

"Pshaw. You don't make me nervous." Ashton began to timorously fiddle with the keychain latched to her beltloop, betraying herself.

"I call your bluff, and I'd love to argue with you since I'd win, but we have to order." Chloe tipped her head towards the checkout counter, where a barista with long, coral colored hair and snakebite piercings was awaiting them.

Ashton smiled at the barista. *When did we get to the front of the line?*

"What do you want?" Chloe asked.

"Medium iced coffee. Black. No sugar."

"Do you want something to eat? You missed breakfast."

Awe. She noticed my absence. "I'm not that hungry." Ashton's stomach rumbled in rebellion.

"You should eat."

"Will that make you happy?" Ashton asked.

"Yes."

"I'll have a blueberry scone then."

Chloe grinned. "Stellar." She pointed to the dining area of the café. "Why don't you go find us a table. I'll place the order."

"I have money, though."

"I got this," Chloe said. "You can buy next time. Now go grab a table please."

"Next time?"

Chloe rolled her eyes and chuckled. "Table. Go."

"Okay. I'm going." Ashton turned and started for the table left of the stage that was being abandoned by a group of middle-aged women. Chloe's stare seared into Ashton's backside until Ashton finally sat down and coolly looked up only to see Chloe approaching her, a beverage in each hand and small paper bag tucked under her right arm. She flashed Ashton an impish smirk when she reached the table.

"Is this seat taken?" Chloe asked Ashton.

"Are you always this insufferable?"

Chloe pouted. "Are you always this serious?"

"No."

"No?" Chloe nodded. "Prove it."

"What?"

"Is this seat taken?" Chloe repeated her question, eyeing Ashton expectantly.

Ashton failed to repress her smile and gestured to the chair across from her. "I was reserving it for you."

Chloe brandished a self-satisfied grin. "Gosh. That's awfully kind of you." She placed the iced coffee and tiny bag in front of Ashton. "For you."

"Thank you."

"You're welcome," Chloe said and took the seat opposite of Ashton. She blew on her steaming beverage and then sipped it carefully.

Ashton removed the scone from the bag, broke off a piece and popped in her mouth. After swallowing her food, she drank from the straw protruding from the plastic cup of iced coffee. "Mmmm," she unwittingly hummed.

Chloe giggled. "Hit the spot, huh?"

Ashton's face flared. She didn't dare look at Chloe. "It's good stuff."

"From the sound of it, I've no doubt," Chloe teased.

Ashton's cheeks continued burning. "How do you take your coffee?"

"Are you asking to distract me from watching you or to get to know me?"

Ashton took a long sip of her drink before speaking. "Both."

"Cream and one sugar," Chloe said. "Do you only drink iced coffee?"

Ashton willed her gaze to connect with Chloe's. "No. I usually drink it hot but this is what I was in the mood for."

Chloe nodded and swirled the stirrer in her cup without breaking eye contact. "Why'd you skip breakfast?"

"Pancakes aren't my thing."

"Oh. Okay. So, what is your thing? Brooding in your room."

Ashton shook her head. "I wasn't brooding. I was getting ready for our da–er, social engagement."

Chloe's smiled villainously. "Wow. You almost slipped up and said date."

"But I didn't." Ashton began chewing on another piece of her scone. "Because it's not a date," she said, her mouth full of food.

Chloe snickered. "Could've fooled me what with the way you're elegantly talking and chewing at the same time."

Ashton finished eating and wiped her mouth with a napkin. "Sorry. That was impolite."

"No worries." Chloe sat back in her seat. "Tell me, though, what *is* the difference between a date and social engagement."

"Well," Ashton swished the ice in her cup around to buy time, "a date would be two people who are romantically interested in each other going out together because they are romantically interested in each other." Ashton rested her elbows on the table and slowly tore her napkin in half, ruminating. "And a social engagement is having plans, such as hanging out with a friend. Platonic stuff. Completely void of romance." She glanced at Chloe. "You know?"

Chloe pursed her lips. "And we're doing the latter?"

"Yes! Exactly."

Chloe placed arms on the table as Ashton had just done. She folded her hands in front of her and leaned forward. Her face was a breath away from Ashton's.

Ashton stilled, her heart hammering with incredible speed. The napkin dropped from her grip.

Chloe's eyes searched Ashton's features before settling on Ashton's dumbfounded stare. Chloe held Ashton's gaze. "What if I told you that when you speak, I watch your mouth and I think about what it would feel like to kiss you? Would that make this a date...since it crosses my mind to be more than platonic with you?" Chloe's voice was low and smooth.

Ashton's heart stalled altogether and collapsed against her ribcage. She tightened her jaw and said nothing while her lungs struggled for oxygen. After she managed the slightest inhale, Ashton responded in a whisper, "I would have to reciprocate."

"And do you?"

"It doesn't matter."

"Of course it matters," Chloe said.

"No, it doesn't." Ashton blinked intentionally then continued. "Because even if I felt those same feelings, I wouldn't date you."

Chloe flinched as if stung by Ashton's words. "Why not? Does it have to do with my being pansexual?"

"Not at all," Ashton said resolutely.

"Does it have to with us having the same last name?"

Ashton's expression squinched up. "Uh...um...yeah. There's that detail. Yup." She sighed laboriously. "Alright the reality that you're my step-sister is kind of—"

"Kinky," Chloe offered with a small smirk.

"Nope. That's not...no. I was going to go for something more along the lines of peculiar."

"Hmm. Okay. I respect your viewpoint, but the actuality of our situation is that we're not biologically related. We're two people who wound up in a blended family," Chloe said. "Hence, if we dated, it wouldn't be incest."

"I know it wouldn't be incest, but that doesn't take away from it being uber weird and borderline scandalous."

"Ashton, I get that our circumstances are...unique, but it's a far cry from scandalous."

"Is it though?" Ashton asked as Noah's cautionary words rang between her ears.

"Yes."

"Well I disagree with you," Ashton said. "I think there are some implicit boundaries here that shouldn't ever be crossed."

Chloe released a sharp exhale of disappointment. "You do?"

Suddenly, a wave of regret washed over Ashton and her chest became heavy. "I do. And if that weren't the case about the boundaries, I *still* wouldn't date you."

Chloe pushed her tongue against the inside of her cheek to camouflage her frown. "Why? Am I not your type?"

"It's got nothing to do with you, it's me," Ashton assured. "I don't date."

Chloe looked askance at Ashton. "What do you mean you don't date?"

"I mean I don't date. Plain and simple," Ashton said.

"Why don't you date?"

"It's complicated."

"I thought it was plain and simple."

"Um. It is, buuut it's also complicated."

"Oh-kay. Then uncomplicate it for me."

"Chloe, can we please talk about something else? Please." The distress in Ashton's voice was perceptible to both girls. Mortified, Ashton went to move her arms, but Chloe was too fast. She covered Ashton's hands with her own. Reflexively, Ashton recoiled and Chloe let go.

"Hey, it's okay," Chloe said softly. "I'm not going to hurt you."

Ashton nodded, unconvinced.

"I have an idea," Chloe said. "Let's get out of this place."

"We don't have to leave."

Chloe stood up. "Yeah, but a change of scenery could be nice. We can talk about whatever you want to talk about." She smiled at Ashton. "What say you? Are you in?"

Ashton stared down at the crumbs of scone on the paper bag and her almost-empty iced coffee cup. She looked up at Chloe and shyly smiled back at her. “I’m in.”

Chapter Eight

Ashton eased out of the passenger side of the SUV and closed the door behind her as she observed the surrounding scenery, which included an assortment of trees, a small body of water, and a stone bench.

"What is this place?" Ashton asked.

Chloe walked over to where Ashton was and stood by her side. Their shoulders brushed and Ashton opened her mouth to breathe a calming breath, but a mouthful of the humid air got lodged in her throat.

"This is Munro Reservation. It's where I come to escape the world," Chloe said. "Do you like it?"

Ashton stared up at the forestry towering above her and Chloe, enclosing them in a secluded enclave of nature. "It's beautiful."

Chloe smiled. "I know." She pointed to the treetops. "They're mostly maple, oak, and pine trees." Then she tipped her head a little, gesturing to their left at the placid pool of liquid. "And that's one of the two fresh water lakes located within this seven hundred acre forest."

"This is great." Ashton looked to the sky, closed her eyes, and let the hot sun caress her face for a long second before turning to Chloe. "Thank you for taking me here."

Chloe nodded. "You're welcome." She motioned with her thumb to the bench. "Wanna sit?"

"Okay," Ashton said and followed Chloe to the stone seat. In silence, both girls sat down and admired the water in front of them. After a lasting moment, Ashton finally spoke. "Did you mean what you said at The Bean?"

"Regarding?"

Ashton inhaled. "That you think about kissing me."

"Yes."

"What about your boyfriend, Trevor? I heard you mention him at lunch yesterday."

Chloe blew out a chuckle. She faced Ashton, but Ashton kept her attention on the lake. "Trevor's not my boyfriend. He's a guy I go on dates with sometimes."

Ashton dipped her head down and away from Chloe to conceal her fallen expression. "Oh." She placed her hand on her knees. "So it's like an open relationship that you have with him, where you can kiss other people?"

"Sort of," Chloe said. "It's not really a relationship. Trevor and I go out. Once in a while, we hook-up, but we both have the freedom to date other people. Relationships aren't something I do. I prefer to date around."

Ashton raised her head enough to see the water again. "Why's that? Do you not believe in monogamy?"

"No. I believe in monogamy. I just don't partake in it."

"Why?"

Chloe laughed. "Wow. You're full of questions, aren't you?"

"Sorry," Ashton mumbled.

"Don't be. It's alright. I've got nothing to hide. I'm just not used to being interrogated."

"Hey!" Ashton quickly turned to confront Chloe, who was grinning. Without any forethought, Ashton gave Chloe a playful push. "I'm not interrogating you!"

Chloe's laugh died out as she caught Ashton by her wrist. The two girls stared at each other soundlessly, but only for a fraction of a minute before Ashton yanked her hand back. "Don't." Ashton's voice was firm.

Chloe held up her open palms, surrendering. "I'm sorry."

Ashton shook her head. "You don't have to apologize. I'm jumpy, that's all."

"Okay."

"So you were saying that you don't partake in monogamy and you were about to tell me why," Ashton said.

Chloe arched an eyebrow at Ashton. "Oh? Is that what I was about to do?"

"Yup."

Chloe smiled. "Well." She cleared her throat. "Unlike yourself, I enjoy dating, but I don't want to be restricted to being with only one person. I favor having options," Chloe said. "Which is why non-monogamous dating is how I roll."

"Don't you think it sounds nice to share experiences with a singular, special someone?"

"Aww. That's a romantic notion, but no. It doesn't sound nice. Frankly, it sounds terrifying."

"How come?" Ashton inquired.

Chloe squinted and pursed her lips. "Tell ya what," she said. "I'll answer that question if you answer one of my questions. Deal?"

Ashton's nose crinkled in aversion. "Fiiine. Deal, but I already know what you are going to ask and the reason I don't date is because I do want a relationship...with only one person. It might seem idealistic or corny, but in spite of my past with—" Ashton waved her hand in front of her face, erasing the thoughts she was about to verbalize. "Never mind." She tucked a strand of her espresso colored hair behind her right ear. "What I'm getting at is that I want to fall in love." A blush scorched Ashton's cheeks and she glimpsed up at the cloudless sky, quietly begging the sun to obscure it.

Chloe gave Ashton a lopsided smile. "That is very idyllic-sounding, but it's also very sweet."

Ashton's surprised gaze fell back upon Chloe. "Really?"

"Really." Chloe nodded. "And I appreciate you sharing all that, but it's not the question I was going to ask."

"It isn't?" Ashton gasped.

"No, ma'am.

"God damnit," Ashton muttered.

Chloe laughed.

"Why'd you let me ramble?" Ashton asked.

"I like listening to your voice. You got a little southern twang going on there."

"That is so not true!"

"You keep telling yourself that," Chloe said with a smirk.

"Aargh!" Ashton covered her face in her hands.

"Awe. No need to be bashful."

"Not helping," Ashton grumbled against her palms.

"Okay. I'm totally done ragging on you. I swear on my life," Chloe said. "Will you look at me?"

Slowly, Ashton moved her hands from her face and raised her eyes to meet Chloe's. The intensity of Chloe's stare struck Ashton with immediate force. Her heart began thumping erratically.

"Hi." Chloe smiled.

"Hi."

"Has anyone ever told you that your eyes are stunning?"

Ashton pouted, her cheeks on fire. "Are you hitting on me again?"

Chloe laughed lightly. "Nah, that's too unoriginal for my style. I'm genuinely curious. At first I thought they were blue, but here, in the sunlight, I see that they're more of a gray color."

"They are gray," Ashton confirmed. "It's rare. I inherited them from my grandpa on my mom's side."

"Stunning."

Ashton couldn't keep from smiling. "You said that already."

"I know because I meant it." Chloe smiled back.

"Well, thank you."

"You're welcome." Chloe's stare sharpened. Ashton drew in a breath, but could not exhale. "Having such a rare eye color must make *you* a rare find," Chloe said. "So I guess I'd be wise to hold onto you." She winked.

"Alright. *That* was flirting!"

Chloe grinned. "You're learning."

"And you're forgetting," Ashton upbraided. "Boundaries."

"Oh yeah. Those." Chloe let out a small cough. "Do I get to ask you my question now?"

"Bring it on."

"What is your chocolate of choice: dark or milk?"

Ashton scowled at Chloe. "Seriously? That's what you were going to originally ask me?"

"It sure was."

"If you must know, it's dark."

Chloe dramatically clasped the signature pendant around her neck and pressed it to her chest. "Oh! Be still, my soul! A woman after my own heart."

Ashton giggled. "That was a lovely performance."

Chloe placed her right arm over her stomach and her left behind her. She bowed.

Ashton shook her head, but continued smiling. "I'm gonna go out a limb here and guess that dark chocolate's where it's at for you as well."

Chloe grinned. "Your guesswork would be accurate, but more importantly do you realize what this makes us?"

Ashton's brow creased quizzically. "I haven't got a clue."

"Spirit animals!" Chloe clapped her hands together.

Ashton gave Chloe a questionable look. "Does it though?"

"Absolutely!"

Ashton nodded. "You keep telling yourself that," she recited Chloe's words from earlier and smirked.

Chloe laughed. "Ahh! Well played." She raised her left hand. "High five!"

Ashton rolled her eyes and reluctantly tapped her palm against Chloe's.

Chloe grimaced. "Alright so that was weak as fuck. We'll practice."

Ashton stuck her tongue out at Chloe. "Whatever. I answered your question so you have to answer mine because we made a deal."

"We did indeed."

"Why does the idea of monogamy terrify you?"

"Different people choose to be non-monogamous for different reasons, and my reason is...mine," Chloe said. "I'm going to answer you truthfully, but I don't want your pity. Okay?"

"Okay."

A somber expression cast over Chloe's face. She ran her fingers through her ultra-pale blonde hair, deeply exhaled, and shrugged lightly. "My mom loved my dad. He was her everything," Chloe said softly. "I was five years old when he died, and I watched my mom fall apart." A short, bitter laugh escaped her throat. "She wouldn't even get out of bed to help me get ready for school. My Aunt Jillian had to move in with us to take care of me. It was like my mom became this empty shell of a person because she didn't have my dad anymore." Chloe's eyes glittered with unshed tears. "I never want to experience that–what my mom went through. She gave her whole heart; her whole self to my dad and in the end, it destroyed her. There's no way I'm going to make that same mistake. I'm not giving all of myself to one person. Nobody gets to have that kind of power over me." She shook her head. "I'll give pieces of my heart to people so then if they break what I gave them, it's only a piece. It's not all that I am." Chloe looked straight into Ashton's sympathetic gaze. "I know my logic might seem fucked up, but—"

"No." Ashton gingerly rested her hand on Chloe's forearm. Both girls stiffened. The blood in Ashton's veins sped through her body and she slightly shivered. Chloe glanced down at Ashton's touch for a lengthy second before her eyes found Ashton's face again. "It makes sense." Ashton spoke quietly. "I get it."

Chloe produced a sad smile.

"I'm sorry about your dad," Ashton said.

"Thank you."

Ashton nodded.

A mild breeze rustled the leaves of the encompassing trees.

"You might not want to hear this," Chloe started. "I can't even imagine how bad your life sucked when Dean left your mother, but in some way, he saved mine. I'm not condoning his or my mom's actions, but he's been good to me and my mom. He's a decent man and he loves you and Noah; talks about you guys all the time."

Slowly, Ashton pulled her hand away from Chloe's. "Right."

"It's just that I lost my dad, but yours is here."

Ashton extracted her phone from the front pocket of her jeans and peered at its screen. "It's getting late. We should probably go." She stood up from the stone bench.

"Ashton, I wasn't trying to upset you by telling you that."

"I'm not upset." The lie tasted bitter spilling from Ashton's mouth. "Can we go please?"

"Yeah. We can go."

Chapter Nine

"What were you girls up to today?" Mr. Daniels asked Ashton and Chloe, who were seated across from him at the long, oval dinner table.

"Coffee and sight-seeing," Chloe said, cutting into the piece of steak on the plate in front of her.

"Wonderful!" Mr. Daniels smiled at Ashton. "Did you enjoy yourself?"

Ashton stabbed a broccoli floret with her fork. "Yeah, it was cool."

"Obviously she enjoyed herself; she had incredible company." Chloe grinned and bumped her knee against Ashton's beneath the table.

Noah coughed into his fist, half chuckling.

Ashton glared at her brother sitting at the opposite side of the table next to her father. Noah smirked and took a drink from his glass of lemonade. Ashton shifted uncomfortably in her chair, moving her left leg further away from Chloe's right leg. She forged a smile in her father's direction then quietly proceeded to eat.

"Where did you venture out to?" Regina asked Chloe.

"The usual." Chloe gave a small shrug of her shoulders. "Strip clubs, sex toy shops, an underground orgy," she said nonchalantly.

Ashton paled and began choking on her mouthful of roasted potatoes. Noah laughed. Regina slammed her palm on the table and pointed the knife in her other hand at Chloe.

"Young lady!" Regina barked. "Need I remind that that kind of talk is completely unacceptable especially at the dinner table?"

Chloe barely raised her eyes to Regina. "Sorry, Mom." She then turned to Ashton and gently patted her on the back. "You good?"

Ashton managed to swallow. She nodded and took a sip of water.

"Regina, go easy," Mr. Daniels said in a low voice. "She was just being silly." He looked at Chloe. "No more crude commentary, alright?"

Chloe glanced at Mr. Daniels. "Okay."

For several minutes, the five of them ate in silence.

"So, what'd you do today?" Ashton asked Noah to lessen the awkward tension in the room.

"I went downtown with Dad to the marketplace to get the fine, fresh vegetables you're consuming as we speak." Noah gave Ashton a toothy smile. "You're welcome."

Ashton rolled her eyes at her brother.

Mr. Daniels chuckled then looked at Ashton. "Would you maybe want to spend some time together this week, the two of us?"

Ashton's eyebrows raised in bewilderment. "What for?"

"To catch up," Mr. Daniels said.

Ashton's posture became taut. She scoffed. "You want to compensate for eleven years in a single afternoon?"

Mr. Daniels frowned. "Ashton, that's not what I—"

"Yeah. No." Ashton shook her head. "I'll take a rain check, thanks."

"Ash," Noah whispered.

Ashton rose from her seat and faced Regina. "May I be excused?"

Regina glimpsed charily at Mr. Daniels, who nodded. She then turned to Ashton. "Of course."

"Thanks for dinner," Ashton said and retreated to her bedroom.

***

Ashton was lying on her bedroom floor watching the blades of the ceiling fan spin. The days' events played themselves over in her mind, but the image she kept coming back to was of Chloe closing in on her from across the table at The Bean, confessing that she'd thought about the two of them kissing. Ashton shut her eyes and there she was: Chloe with her dark, soulful eyes, cherry-red lips, and sleek, blonde hair. Ashton's chest locked mid-exhale as the dull ache between her legs began to ripen. Quasi-consciously, Ashton's left hand found its way to the button on her jeans. A knock at the door startled her from her reverie. Ashton quickly sat up, crossed her legs over one another, dug her phone from her pants pocket, and started thumbing through the screens, pretending to read what was in front of her. "Come in," she managed with the most even tone she could muster.

Ashton's bedroom door opened and Noah stepped inside. He glared at his sister then padded slowly towards her.

"What is your problem?" Noah asked in a harsh whisper.

"What is my problem with what?"

"Dad was trying to make a connection with you and you totally gave him the shaft. Why?"

"Ohhh." Ashton nodded. "*That* problem." She met her brother's eyes with her own hardened stare. "Look, I understand. You two are doing the father and son thing and if that's working for you then as your sister, you have my blessing, but I am not going to be daddy's little girl to a man that I legit don't even want to be affiliated with." Ashton spoke through gritted teeth. "He's a liar and a cheater and he bailed on mom. He bailed on us, Noah. So, yeah, I have a problem with him and he is not my dad. He is my biological father and that is all he will ever to be me. Now I'm respecting your relationship with him and I'm asking you to do the same for me."

"You don't have a relationship with him, Ash."

"Exactly and that's how I want to keep it."

Noah sighed and squatted in front of Ashton. "I know you're resentful, but if you carry that around with you for the rest of your life, it's eventually going to eat away at you."

A sharp, jeering sound burst out of Ashton. She pointed her finger at Noah. "Do not fucking preach to me."

"That isn't what I'm do—"

"You act as though you don't remember how mom struggled to make ends meet when we were kids as a single parent or all nights we overheard her crying herself to sleep after our father moved out. You were there, Noah. Those were shitty times, and maybe you can make peace with him and the suffering he caused me, you, and mom, but I'm not going to." Ashton took a breath. "I mean, Jesus, it's difficult enough as it is for me to live under the same roof as the man, but I'm doing it and I'd really appreciate it if you'd expect nothing more from me than to just get through these next three months. Can you do that?"

Noah glimpsed at the floor and exhaled in resignation. "Yes. I can do that."

"Thank you."

Noah lifted his head to face Ashton. Suspicion clouded his blue eyes. "What *did* happen today with you and Chloe?"

"Aargh!" Ashton palmed her forehead. "Nothing."

"Would you tell me if something did happen?"

"Ye—no." Ashton shook her head and looked at Noah. "Because nothing is going to happen."

"Do you want something to happen?"

"Dude, why are you grilling me?"

"You're my twin," Noah said. "I know you and I know she gets to you. You might be able to hide that from everyone else, but I can see it."

"I think you're hallucinating."

"I think you're in denial."

"I think you're fishing; trying to find more things to hold against me," Ashton said.

Noah gasped. "What? I'm not holding anything against you."

"Ha! Really?"

"Honest to god."

"What about the Dean issue?" Ashton asked.

"That's your business and you were right, it's your prerogative to have, or not have, a relationship with him. I'm sorry for riding your ass about it." Noah swallowed. "You're my sister and regardless of what you believe, I *do* have your back."

Ashton half-smiled. "I have your back, too." Her expression quickly morphed into one of uncertainty. "Wait. If you have my back, then why you do keep harping on me about Chloe?"

Noah shrugged. "I want to protect you."

"From what?"

"A world of trouble."

"I don't follow," Ashton said.

Noah rubbed his unshaven chin. "For the hell of it, let's say that Chloe does get to you and you decide to pursue her—"

"Whoa! I'm gonna stop you there."

"I'm not finished. Hear me out, will ya?"

Ashton squinted. "Grrrr. Fine. Finish."

"If you two got involved with one another..." Noah cringed. "I'm really trying to have a wicked open mind here so bear with me." He coughed. "If you got involved with Chloe, I would never disown you. I *would* have your back...even though it'd be fucking weird, but I digress. I'm thinking mom, dad, and Regina might have a few grievances with that sorta...er...phenomenon. It could cause pandemonium within the family. They might reject you, and you'd wind up getting hurt." Noah frowned. "Ashton, I've seen you hurt enough, and I wasn't able to protect you before, but now...I don't know. At least I can say something; give you a warning."

Ashton nodded, digesting her brother's appeal. "Finished?"

"Yes."

Ashton pursed her lips. "I don't want to fight with you."

"I don't want to fight with you either."

"Then you hear me out, okay?"

"Okay."

"I appreciate this brotherly love thing that you're doing here. I do. But I don't need your protection, Noah."

"Ashton, last time—"

"Shh. No." Ashton shook her head emphatically. "Calm yourself. Nothing is going to happen between me and Chloe. It's not like that with us."

"Then how is it?"

Ashton's eyebrows drew together. "Um. It's...we're building a friendship," she said, privately second-guessing the verity of her answer.

"A friendship, eh?"

"Yup."

"Okay." Noah stood up and walked to the door. He paused before exiting and glanced back at Ashton. "Does Chloe know that?" He posed his question and left.

Chapter Ten

Ashton paced the hallway in front of Chloe's closed bedroom door. She rehearsed her lines under her breath, "Hey, what's shaking?" She winced and shook her head. "So, I thought we should have a chat about our budding friendship." *Budding? Really?* She frowned.

"Wow. You *do* talk to yourself often." Chloe's voice came from behind. Ashton's heart tripped and she stopped in her tracks, inwardly cringing. She blinked purposefully then slowly turned around.

Chloe was standing on the top stair, one hand on the banister, her mouth curled into a grin, her eyes fixed on Ashton.

Ashton's abdomen tightened and burned at the sight of Chloe. "Hi. I didn't know you were there."

"Evidently." Chloe stepped onto the second floor landing. She pointed to her bedroom. "You thought I was in there?"

"Yes. Yes, I did."

Chloe glanced at the chic, black watch on her wrist. She pursed her lips. "It's eleven o' clock." Her eyes found Ashton's again. "Come for a late night visit?"

Ashton thrust her hands into the pockets of her jeans to furtively dry her sweat-sticky palms. "In a way," Ashton said. "Can we talk?"

"Sure." Chloe strode towards Ashton and reached past her for the brass doorknob. A breath of Chloe's fresh, sweet scent filled Ashton's nose and her lungs locked. She swallowed hard as Chloe opened the door. "After you." Chloe motioned with her right arm to the bed in the center of the room.

Ashton nodded and anxiously scanned the environment for a place to sit other than the bed. The chair by the desk was occupied by a heap of laundry.

Ashton's gaze inadvertently caught sight of a lacey, lilac purple thong atop of the pile. A rush of heat infused her cheeks with a deep shade of scarlet. Butterflies flitted in her belly. She hurriedly looked away, assuming engrossment in the random stack of CDs on the second shelf of Chloe's overcrowded bookcase. "I think I'll just stand," Ashton said, her back to Chloe.

The click of the bedroom door closing was faint. "Do you as you please," Chloe said. "So what would you like to chat about?"

Ashton wound around to face Chloe. "You still listen to compact discs?"

Chloe glimpsed over at her CDs then smiled at Ashton. "Yeah. I'm retro like that."

Ashton returned the smile. "Cool."

Chloe's eyes carefully regarded Ashton from head to toe, taking in the full scope of Ashton's body.

Ashton internally squirmed beneath the weight of Chloe's stare. Her heart thundered in her chest. She was certain she was going to faint from a lack of air.

Chloe's gaze finally fell in with Ashton's. She bit her bottom lip and smirked. Ashton's knees became wobbly but she was able to quietly let go of a belated exhale.

"You rock those skinny jeans," Chloe said. "I meant to tell you earlier."

Ashton pressed her lips together in a leery smile. "Are you flirting? Because boundaries."

Chloe gaped, exaggeratingly. "Would *I* push the boundaries and flirt with you?"

"Maybe."

Chloe grinned deviously. "Guilty as charged." She crossed her arms over her chest. "But honestly, I was just paying you a compliment right then."

"Okay." Ashton nodded. "Well, thank you."

"You're welcome." Chloe tipped her head to side a bit. "What did you want to chat about?"

"This."

Chloe's brow wrinkled. "This what?"

"This thing we're doing."

Chloe's eyes glimmered with mischief. "We're doing a thing?"

"Ye—no...er...I mean...ugh!" Ashton shook her head. "Yes. We are. We're developing a friendship," she said. "And I needed to make sure that you knew that that's all this is–our thing–it's a friendship."

"A friendship. Gotcha." Chloe sauntered towards Ashton.

Ashton swallowed with great effort as beads of perspiration began to collect between her shoulder blades. Chloe stopped only when the tips of her ankle boots touched the white, rubber caps of Ashton's sneakers.

"Then can I ask you a friendly question?" Chloe spoke softly.

"Alright."

"Are you nervous?"

Ashton inhaled. "Is that the question?"

"Nope. That was the prequel to the question."

"Honestly?" Ashton asked.

"Honestly."

"A little. I'm a little nervous."

"Why?"

"Because you make me—nothing. Never mind. Please ask me the friendly question," Ashton said.

"Can you keep a secret?"

Ashton gave Chloe a suspicious look. "That's the question?"

"It is."

"Yeah. I can keep a secret."

"Good." Chloe slowly closed in on Ashton. Ashton's heart dipped into her belly and she stopped breathing. Their cheeks brushed and suddenly, Chloe's mouth was lightly touching Ashton's earlobe. "I know you just want us to be friends. I respect that," she whispered. "But friend to friend, you should know that I have a major crush on you." Chloe's lips grazed the left side of Ashton's face in a gentle peck. Ashton quivered and became dizzy as Chloe backed up. The loss of Chloe's nearness caused a short, cold sting against Ashton's skin.

Chloe stared at Ashton, unsmiling. "Is there anything you want to share with me?"

Ashton shook her head, stupefied.

The edges of Chloe's mouth turned downward and she dropped her gaze, nodding. In seconds, she recovered from her discouraged state and looked at Ashton. She tucked a few strands of her longish bangs behind her ear while taking another step back. "Alright then," she said. "Well, if you change your mind, I can keep a secret too."

"Thanks," Ashton said.

"No worries." Chloe shrugged. "That's what friends do, is it not?"

"It is."

"And we're friends. Are we not?"

Ashton eyed Chloe circumspectly. "We are."

"Then there you have it. We're friends...and nothing more because that's what you want, right?" Chloe inquired.

Ashton's gut wrenched. "Right." She gave Chloe a flimsy smile. "Thanks for your time," Ashton said and started towards the exit with an unsteady gait.

"Hey, Ashton?" Chloe called after her.

Ashton opened the door and glanced back to face Chloe. "Yeah?"

"Do me a favor, will ya, *pal*?"

"What?"

"Don't forget what I said about Dean being a good man," Chloe said.

"I won't."

"Really? Cuz you could have fooled me at dinner."

Ashton glared at Chloe. "Goodnight," she said and walked out of Chloe's bedroom.

Chapter Eleven

A melodic chime roused Ashton from a deep slumber. She groaned into her pillow and slowly rolled over on the mattress, getting herself twisted up in the sheets. She rubbed the sleep from her eyes until they finally came into focus. Groggily, she reached for the tablet on her bedside table. A video call request from Katlyn appeared on the screen. Ashton propped herself up into a pseudo-seated position and hit the "accept" button on the device.

Katlyn's face popped up. "Wakey, wakey, sleepy head," she said in a sing-song tone. Her mellow-brown eyes were wide, matching the cheerful expression she wore.

"Ugh. Dude, what time is it?"

"It's 6:09 in the a.m." Katlyn grinned. "Good morning!"

"Yeah. Morning to you, too," Ashton grumbled. "Why on earth are you calling me at this hour? Why are you even awake? And why are you so chipper?"

Katlyn rolled her eyes. "Oh, puh-lease! You used to get up at the crack-ass of dawn regularly for track meets."

"Right, but those days are behind me now as you well know, which begs the question: what's this about?"

"I'll beg you a question, you dork." Katlyn laughed. "Do you know what today is?"

Ashton squinted at the date on the bottom corner of her tablet. "Wednesday. The fifteenth of June."

"Exactly!" Katlyn squealed. "It's the launch date for our favorite violinist's tour!"

Ashton gasped. "Oh. My. God. Is that why you're conscious this early? For ticket sales? Kat, did you score tickets to see Eliza Diamonds?! Tell me you did!"

"I did!"

Ashton threw fist in the air. "Yasss! That's the raddest!" She shook her head, smiling. "Damn. I'm ridiculously envious of you right now. You have to take pictures for me, okay?"

Katlyn laughed. "I'll admit, it is way rad, but the thing is, *you'll* be the one taking pictures for *me*."

"What? I don't understand."

"Hello, featherbrain! I got the tickets for you."

Ashton gaped in Ashtonishment. "You did? For me?"

"Yes, for you," Katlyn said. "Eliza's playing an intimate show in Boston at some venue called the Beantown Lounge so I bought two tickets."

Ashton grinned. "Are you coming here to go to the concert with me?"

"Dude, I'm amazing but I'm not that amazing."

Ashton pouted. "If you can't come then why'd you get the tickets?"

"Ash, all you ever talk about is how badly you want to see her perform. It was trending online that she was making an appearance in Boston and it just made sense to me to get you tickets."

Ashton's chest swelled up with emotion. "You didn't have to do that. It's way too generous of a gift."

"I know I didn't have to. I wanted to." Katlyn shrugged. "Consider it a premature birthday present."

"Kat, Thank you! You're the best!"

"Hell yeah, I am." Katlyn giggled. "You're welcome."

Ashton smiled. "I still don't understand why you got two tickets though."

"Dude, are you thick? This way, you don't have to go alone. You offer someone else the other ticket."

"Like who? Noah is very open about his aversion to her music. He won't wanna go with me."

Katlyn's left eyebrow arched, a waggish smirk tugged at her mouth. "Weeel-ll, you could always ask Chloe."

Ashton scoffed. "Kat, must we keep going through this? I told you, Chloe and I have barely spoken to each other for like three weeks now."

"How do you two live in same house, call yourselves friends, and not speak?"

"Easy. It's a big house so our paths don't cross very often and we don't have all that much to say to one another."

"Or." Katlyn held up her index finger. "You're purposely avoiding each other because you both have too much to say to one another. Huh? Huh? Huh? What do you think of that theory?"

"I think that theory sucks ass." Ashton rolled her eyes and exhaled loudly. "But there's a small possibility that it's on point."

"Yes!" Katlyn cheered. "Okay then use the tickets as an ice breaker or a peace offering for when you gave her an attitude, or..." She grinned. "To ask her on a date."

"Ha!" Ashton's cheeks rouged at the thought. "Not gonna happen." She frowned at Kat with her eyes. "I don't want to date and even if I did, I wouldn't date her. We went over this a gazillion times already."

"But we agreed that you guys aren't actually related so your crush on her isn't wrongful and—"

Ashton's eyes enlarged in horror. "Shh! Shoosh!" She scrambled to lower the volume on her tablet. "Holy Christ, Kat! Keep your voice down!" Ashton demanded in a harsh whisper. "When I confided in you about that...about the c-r-u-s-h, you promised never to bring it up again."

A short chuckle escaped Katlyn. "Um. I love you, Ash, but I'm pretty sure everyone you live with can spell excluding the baby. Furthermore, my friend, I didn't break the promise because the promise was that I not to tell anyone, and I haven't." She stuck her tongue out Ashton.

"Aargh! Well, can you promise now to never bring it up again?"

"No."

Ashton gasped. "Why not?"

"Because if we don't talk about it as though it's some big taboo, then we give it power; we make it a taboo and it isn't a taboo," Katlyn said. "You're making this way harder than it has to be."

"Once more, dude, taboo or not, I would never ask Chloe on a date. She's undateable."

Katlyn's brow wrinkled. "Please define for me what the fuck 'undateable' is."

"I told you before. Chloe doesn't date with the intent to get involved in a relationship. She dates non-monogamously. She wants to steer clear of relationships," Ashton said. "If ever the world turned upside down and I *did* decide to date, I *would* date with the intention of it eventually evolving into a relationship."

Katlyn sighed. "And I told YOU that perhaps you should give dating a shot. You've never done it. You might like it. It would allow you to get your romance on without giving your everything to just one person like the way you did with that demon bitch that shan't be named."

"You sound just like Chloe when you talk about dating that way." Ashton shook her head. "And Fel—she who shall remain nameless isn't a demon."

Katlyn's jaw dropped. "How can you defend her?! She hurt you...deliberately. That makes her a demon in my book. What the hell book are you reading?"

"I worked really hard in therapy to forgive her. It was the only way I could even try to move passed it," Ashton said. "I'm not coming to her defense. I'm just telling you that she isn't a demon."

"You're a better person than I'll ever be. I still want to introduce her face to my fists."

Ashton pressed her lips together in a sad smile. "I know." She took a deep breath. "New subject please."

"Alright." Katlyn nodded. "How's about you take the idea of asking Chloe to the show with you and sit on it? The concert is next month. You've got plenty of time to ponder. Whatdya say?"

"If I sit on it, will you lay off the topic for awhile?"

"How long is awhile?"

"Jesus."

"I hear your prayer," Katlyn said through a laugh. "Fine. I'll back off a bit, but only if you seriously think about it."

"Alright. Yes. I'll seriously think about it."

"You make me proud, Daniels."

"I said I'll think about it. I didn't say I'd do anything."

"However, if you did do it, that would be a most fantabulous way to thank me for the gift." Katlyn smirked.

"Really? You're going to try to play that card?"

"That's not a question. I *am* playing that card."

"I hate you."

"You love me."

Ashton glared at Katlyn but cracked a smile within seconds. "True story."

Chapter Twelve

The fully risen sun shone brightly down on the dewy, morning grass of the local high school's field, surrounded by a newly paved running track. The humidity had yet to set in making the air light and crisp. Ashton put her hands on her hips and slowly bent her body to the left then to the right as she came to the end of her five-minute stretch. She lowered herself closer to the ground and placed one foot near the starting line. She trained her sights on the 400 meters of asphalt before her, took several controlled breaths, and began running. Ashton's toned legs carried her at a moderate pace for the first lap around the track and then she broke into a sprint. As she picked up speed, droplets of sweat started to trickle from the hairline of her tight ponytail down the sides of her face. When Ashton set out on a third lap, she reduced the velocity at which she raced once again until she was steadily jogging. She rounded the course a fourth time before finally stopping at the spray painted, white finish line. She inhaled through clenched teeth, swiped the back of her right hand across her dripping forehead then leaned forward and held onto her kneecaps while she waited for her breathing to regulate. After a few minutes passed, Ashton stood and with the guidance of the map on her phone's GPS, she started trekking in the direction of the house whence she came.

***

Ashton twisted the key in the lock and opened the front door to her father's house. The smell of burnt toast accompanied by the clanking of dishware and various conversing voices struck her senses before she even passed through the entrance. Ashton quietly shut the door behind her and stepped into the foyer.

The dining room was to her left and the stairs were straight ahead. She glanced over at everyone sitting around the large, wooden table. They were all engaged. Apparently her arrival went unnoticed due to the morning commotion. She got a firmer grip on the paper coffee cup in her right hand and began tip toeing towards the staircase. Suddenly, the sound of her name followed by a deafening ring of silence stopped her mid-step.

"Welcome back," Chloe said. "Join us for breakfast?"

"Yeah. There's coffee." Noah added.

Ashton grit her teeth, cleared her throat, and turned to face the three pairs of eyes now staring at her. She pressed her lips into a tight smile and gave the onlookers a nod of acknowledgment. She lifted the cup in her hands so that it was in their sights. "I'm all set. Thanks though."

"Have you eaten?" Mr. Daniels asked.

"No."

"Then come have something," her father offered. "We have toast, scrambled eggs, and fruit salad."

Ashton glanced at Noah whose blue eyes shot her an urging look.

"Okay," Ashton said and slowly walked to the table. The heat of Chloe's gaze scalded her. Ashton wordlessly wished that she was wearing more than just a racerback tanktop and spandex capris. She glimpsed at Chloe, who was smirking between bites of fruit salad as she shamelessly ogled Ashton, who blushed fiercely in response and looked away. All at once, Ashton's awareness of her over exposed body heightened. Her thoughts raced. *Shit! Please don't let them notice.* Ashton casually pulled out the chair across from Chloe and sat down. There was already an empty plate on the placemat in front of her. She set her coffee cup next to it.

Regina handed Ashton a bowl with a ladle sticking out of it. "Your dad made the eggs using his special recipe."

Ashton took the bowl. "Awesome," she said dryly as she scooped eggs onto her dish. She placed the bowl on the table and reached for a slice of toast from the small basket at the table's center. Afterwards, she picked up the large, glass dish filled with diced melon, strawberries, blueberries, and kiwi, helping herself to a liberal spoonful of fruit salad. She jabbed the eggs with her fork and began eating.

Noah nudged Ashton with his elbow. "The eggs are the bomb, aren't they?"

With her mouthful of food, Ashton gave her father a thumbs up. Mr. Daniels grinned proudly and Regina smiled.

"I gather you went for a run," Noah said to Ashton.

Ashton swallowed. "Yeah. I was up early and couldn't get back to sleep so I walked to the track."

"You walked?" Mr. Daniels asked. "That's well over a mile."

Ashton shrugged. "It's fine. It was a good warm-up."

"The keys to the family SUV are on the kitchen counter by the fridge," Mr. Daniels said. "Feel free to drive next time. Just be sure to leave a note."

"Thanks." Ashton inhaled and stared at her plate. "I appreciate that."

Beneath the table, Chloe tapped her foot against Ashton's. Ashton looked up quickly at Chloe, who gave her a nod and a smile that caused her pulse to accelerate. Ashton reciprocated the smile and lifted her coffee cup to her mouth.

"I see you found your way to The Bean," Chloe said.

Ashton took a sip. "I sure did."

Chloe squinted at the cup in Ashton's hand. "What's all over your cup?"

Ashton placed her drink on the table. "I was chatting with the barista. She was friendly. I guess she felt like decorating my cup."

The line between Chloe's eyes deepened. "With her phone number and a bunch of heart shapes?" Her tone carried with it an iota of envy.

Mr. Daniels and Regina chuckled.

Ashton smirked. "Jealous?" She mouthed to Chloe and continued eating.

Chloe rolled her eyes and shook her head.

"Well done, sis!" Noah patted Ashton's shoulder. "You should call her."

"No," Ashton said.

"Why not?" Chloe pointed to Ashton's cup. "I believe that's Jocelyn's artwork. She's fun. Noah's right. You should call her."

Ashton choked on the blueberry making its way down her throat. She beat her chest with her fist as she coughed.

"Are you alright?" Mr. Daniels asked, pushing his chair from the table, about to get up.

Ashton raised her hand. "I'm good. I'm good." She looked at Chloe. "You know her?"

"Do I know who? Jocelyn?" Chloe pursed her lips. "Yeah. You could say that," she said with a wink.

Ashton glowered at Chloe.

"Jealous?" Chloe soundlessly back talked.

Ashton's jaw became rigid and she scoffed at Chloe.

Noah's eyes bounced from Chloe to Ashton. He clipped his elbow against his sister's. "Ahem."

Ashton peered over at Noah, who quietly cautioned her with a cold stare before speaking airily, "Hey, Ash, I was thinking we could do an Instavisit with Mom sometime soon. You down?"

"Sure. I'm down." She bit into her toast.

"So," Mr. Daniels spoke up. "Regina and I made reservations for this Friday night at the new Indian restaurant that opened in the theater district and Kristen had to cancel, leaving us in need of someone to watch Ariel," he said. "I thought I'd ask the three of you about your availability and if you all already have plans, that's no problem. We'll change our reservations."

"Is Kristen the nanny?" Noah asked.

"Yes," Regina confirmed.

"I can't," Chloe said. "I've got a date."

Ashton's stomach knotted, but she didn't say anything.

"With Trevor?" Regina asked Chloe.

"No. With Erin."

Mr. Daniels took a contemplative sip from his coffee mug. "Who's Erin?"

"A girl I met online."

Another sharp streak of jealousy ripped through Ashton. Her gut wrenched even more. She couldn't bring herself to look at Chloe.

Noah winced. "Sorry, Dad. I have a date too."

Ashton's fork fell from her hand and quickly turned to face her brother. She gaped at Noah. "You do?"

Noah grinned. "I totally do."

"Who are you going on a date with?"

"Her name is Lily. We met that night at Mercury," Noah said. "We exchanged numbers and have kept in touch, but we're actually going out together Friday."

"Way to go." Chloe smiled at Noah.

"Why didn't you tell me this?" Ashton asked Noah.

Noah gave a small shrug. "I was going to eventually."

"Eventually?" Ashton repeated. "Thanks a lot, bro."

"What about you?" Mr. Daniels asked Ashton.

Ashton glanced at her father. "What about me?"

"Do you have plans Friday night?"

Ashton picked her fork back up and used it to push around the food on her plate. "Nothing concrete yet," she spoke softly.

"How do you feel about filling in for Kristen and spending some time with your baby sister?" Mr. Daniels asked.

Ashton shifted uncomfortably in her seat, trapped under Chloe's watchfulness. She inhaled through her nose and swallowed. She glimpsed at Regina then her father. "Okay."

Mr. Daniels clapped his hands together. "Excellent!" He stood from his chair. "I have to get to work," he announced and gave Regina a peck on her cheek. "I'll see you all later." He grinned at Ashton. "Thank you, Ashton."

"You're welcome, Dean," Ashton replied and as she turned back to her half-eaten breakfast, Chloe caught her eye. Their stares locked for a moment and Chloe awarded Ashton with a soft smile, which somehow made Ashton's begrudging attempt at being kind to her father completely worth it.

Chapter Thirteen

"I'm so happy to see you both!" Mrs. Daniels exclaimed on the other end of the computer screen. "I miss you guys!"

"It's good to see you, too," Ashton said. "How's Florida?"

"Hot and sunny with the occasional rainstorm. The usual." Mrs. Daniels smiled. "Enough about Florida. Tell me how Boston is."

"I'm a fan," Noah said.

"That's because you met a girl," Ashton stated.

Mrs. Daniels gaped. "Noah, you met a girl?!"

"Yeah," Ashton snapped. "And he failed to mention it to me. He's been keeping it on the down low for weeks."

Noah gave Ashton a quick shove to the side, but she grabbed onto the edge of Noah's mattress, where they were sitting, to stabilize herself. "Ma, it's not like that," Noah started. "I met her and we talked a few times but I didn't know if it was going to become something more, which is why I didn't say anything."

"I'm your kin." Ashton drove her index finger against Noah's chest. "We're twins, dude."

Noah rolled his eyes. "I know we shared a womb yada yada, but I'm still not going to tell you everything that happens in my life."

Ashton sneered at her brother. "You don't have to be a jerkface about it."

"Ha!" Noah shook his head. "I'm not a jerkface. You are."

"Kids! Stop!" Mrs. Daniels shouted.

Ashton and Noah immediately became quiet.

"Thank you," Mrs. Daniels said. "Alright. So, you met a girl, Noah. That's wonderful." She aimed her attention at Ashton. "What about you, Ash? Have you met anyone? Made any new friends?"

"Nope. I'm happy flying solo."

Mrs. Daniels frowned. "Are you moping around? Because that's negative energy. You don't want to give off negative energy."

"I'm not moping, Mom." Ashton held up her hands. "I swear."

"She's being honest," Noah said to Mrs. Daniels. "She hung out with Chloe once and she even enlisted herself to be Ariel's sitter this Friday."

Mrs. Daniels smiled at her daughter. "Thatta girl!"

Ashton nodded. "Right."

"How was it meeting your other siblings?" Their mother asked.

"Strictly speaking, only Ariel is our sibling," Ashton said. "We're not blood-related to Chloe."

Mrs. Daniels raised her eyebrows. "Okay, but Chloe's still a part of the family."

Noah glared at Ashton. "Told ya so."

Ashton stared at the computer screen while flipping Noah off.

"Ashton!" Mrs. Daniels reprimanded.

Ashton groaned. "Sorry, Mom."

"Don't do it again," Mrs. Daniels said. "Now, please answer my question."

Noah and Ashton exchanged a look then turned towards their mother. "Ariel is super cute," Ashton said.

"And Chloe is really...cool." Noah pursed his lips. "Yeah. She's cool. I'd say that sums her up."

"You're both being safe?" Mrs. Daniels asked.

"Always," Noah assured.

"The living situation is tolerable?" Their mother inquired.

"Totally." Noah grinned.

Mrs. Daniels looked at her daughter. "Ashton?"

"Uh." Ashton shrugged. "Yup. I'm managing."

"I'm glad to hear that and remember, 'family' and 'home' are simply words. You get to define them," Mrs. Daniels said. "Got it?"

"Got it."

"Good." Mrs. Daniels exhaled. "Alrighty, kiddos. I've gotta go. I'll talk to you guys soon. I love you!"

Ashton and Noah simultaneously waved and said, "Love you" to their mother. Then the screen went black.

Chapter Fourteen

Ashton stood in front of her open closet perusing her meager wardrobe to choose an outfit for the day before taking a shower. She went to reach for the straight crop jeans when a knock at her bedroom door brought her to a standstill. "Hello?"

"It's Chloe," the voice outside the room called back. "Can I come in?"

Ashton's heart stammered. She glimpsed down at herself. She hadn't changed yet. Her running clothes hugged her body, revealing far more than she wanted to show Chloe...for a second time. She pulled a hooded sweatshirt off one of the hangers and quickly slipped her arms inside of it. "It's unlocked," Ashton responded.

The bedroom door opened and Chloe stepped through the entrance. She shut the door behind her and glanced to her left at Ashton. "Hey."

Ashton turned to Chloe. "Hi."

Without hesitation, Chloe made her way towards Ashton in measured steps until they were face to face. Ashton held her breath. Chloe had on low-rise jeans that relaxed at her thighs and tapered at the ankles, which were cuffed. Her indigo, short-sleeved, jersey top scooped at the neck, baring her collarbone. Chloe's trademark pendant rested against her chest. Her long bangs were pinned to the side of her head with a snap clip and the rest of her layered, blonde hair hung right above her shoulders. Ashton struggled not to stare at Chloe's shiny, full, red lips. The girls' eyes met and the depth of Chloe's black-brown gaze caused Ashton's belly to stir madly.

"Something I can help you with?" Ashton's voice was low.

"I wanted to tell you that I thought it was cool that you volunteered to babysit." Chloe gave Ashton a lopsided smile. "Like maybe you mulled over the stuff I talked to you about a few weeks ago."

Ashton shrugged. "I might've." She inhaled, but the air was awash in Chloe's scent. Ashton's head became swimmy. "Is that all you came here for? To tell me that."

Chloe's eyes trailed Ashton from top to bottom then back up again. She bit her bottom lip. "Why? What would happen if I came here for more?"

Ashton frowned. "Nothing."

Chloe smirked. "You're cute."

"Thank you." Ashton pointed to the exit. "Will you leave now?"

"No."

Ashton gaped. "What?"

"Why have you been avoiding me ever since that day in my room?"

"That's not...I haven't been," Ashton lied. "I sat across from you at breakfast just this morning. See? I was right there."

"That was hardly your choice. You ate with us out of obligation because you got caught trying to ninja your way upstairs—a clear act of avoidance, and otherwise, you dodge me whenever you can."

"Not true."

"Very true." Chloe exhaled. Ashton could practically taste the mint toothpaste on her breath. "You don't even return my texts."

"You texted me?" Ashton feigned ignorance.

Chloe narrowed her stare, her brow furrowed. "Don't pretend to be oblivious. I texted you twice, but I never heard back from you so I left you alone." She sighed heavily. "What's going on? Please talk to me."

Ashton folded her arms across her chest. "Do you even have time to have a conversation? I mean your schedule must be pretty booked what with Trevor and Erin and Jocelyn."

Chloe pursed her lips. "Is this you admitting you're jealous?"

"Psht. That is so not what this is."

"Uh huh. Well if it's any consolation, *you're* the one Jocelyn made a pass at. Not me."

"Yeah. No. That wasn't comforting in the least bit especially considering that *you've* been with her already."

"Ages ago and now she's interested in you." Chloe rolled her eyes. "Writing her number on your coffee cup." She scoffed. "Such a rookie move."

Ashton shook her head. "She's a fucking barista. It's not like she has a lot to work with."

"Still."

Ashton let out a short, pungent laugh. "Are *you* jealous?"

"Yes!"

Ashton flinched. "Oh," she whispered. "Why?"

"Because." Chloe pouted. "My number is the number I want you calling."

Suddenly, the room was stuffy and cramped. Ashton took off her sweatshirt and flung it onto her bed. "I can't. We can't."

Chloe pursed her lips, clearly suppressing a pleased grin as she eyed Ashton's newly uncovered skin. "Ashton, I'm not asking you to date me. I'm only asking you to hang out with me again; to stop avoiding me. We're supposed to be friends, remember? Friends text each other and call each other and hang out together, right?"

"You're not wrong."

"Then what's the problem?"

"I don't appreciate it when you try to tell me how to navigate things with Dean," Ashton said.

"I'm sorry."

"It's fine. It's done."

"It isn't fine," Chloe said. "I overstepped. I apologize."

Ashton heaved a breath of frustration. "There's more." Her arms relaxed and dropped to her sides. "There's more to why I've been staying away from you; why I didn't text you back."

"Ahh! So you *did* get my texts." Chloe smirked.

Ashton's stare darkened. "Please don't use this moment to gloat."

Chloe's expression sedated. "I'm sorry. I retract my gloating."

"Thank you."

"Of course." Chloe nodded. "Whatever you want to tell me, I'm listening."

A lump rose in Ashton's throat and her gray eyes began to well up.

"Hey, hey, hey. Don't cry." Chloe quickly reached for Ashton's hand and was able to capture it in her own before Ashton could pull back. Ashton's arm jerked in Chloe's grasp and Chloe ran her thumb over Ashton's knuckles. She stepped closer to Ashton. "It's okay. I won't hurt you."

Tears began to streak Ashton's cheeks. "You might. She did."

A shadow of sadness cast across Chloe's features. "Who?" Her eyes roved over Ashton's bare skin until her gaze locked on Ashton's left shoulder. She inspected the scar tissue that formed an uneven line down the backside of Ashton's arm, ending at her elbow. Chloe opened her mouth but didn't speak. With shaky fingers of her free hand, Ashton slipped the left strap of her tank top off, unveiling another jagged, two-inch long mark above her breast. Chloe took in a sharp breath. "Ashton, who did this to you?" Chloe's voice was almost too low to be heard.

"Her name is Felicia. She's my ex." Ashton shook her head. "In the beginning, it was just a slap here and there. It kept escalating though. I don't even remember how. Then one night she wanted to...and I didn't. I didn't want to. I wanted to go home instead. So I went to leave and that really pissed her off. She cracked a beer bottle over my skull; knocked me down. Told me if I was going leave, I couldn't until she left a mark on me that way I'd never forget her...and she did. She used a shard of glass and marked me. Then she bashed my head against the floor." Ashton pressed her lips together to stop them from trembling. Nearly a minute of quiet passed and she spoke again, "I woke up alone. Most of my clothes were gone." She shuddered at the memory. "Eventually, I found my phone and called my best friend. She came to get me." Ashton released a short, poignant laugh. "Felicia was right. I never forgot her." Ashton fixed the strap of her top. "It's gross. I know."

Chloe looked up at Ashton with her own watery eyes. "No. It's not gross. It's horrific and I'm so sorry you had to go through that, but it's not gross. " She relinquished her grip on Ashton and cupped Ashton's face in her palms. "You're beautiful," Chloe whispered, wiping the tears from Ashton's cheeks with the pads of her thumbs.

Ashton's heart tumbled into her stomach. Weak-kneed and dazed by the softness of Chloe's touch and the warmth of her breathy words, Ashton closed her eyes for a prolonged second. She gulped. Finally, her eyelids flickered open. She placed her hands on top of Chloe's and gently lifted Chloe's palms off of her face. Ashton smiled mournfully. "We can't."

"We're not."

"But when you're this near to me, I...nothing." Ashton knit her brows and the edges of her mouth turned down. "Chloe, I've been avoiding you because it's too hard for me to be around you."

Chloe's eyes widened, a glint of knowing flashed across them. "Why?"

"You get to me."

Chloe scraped her bottom lip with her top teeth. "I get to you how?"

Ashton scowled. "Do you really need me to say it?"

"No. I don't *need* you say it, but I really want you to."

Ashton respired deeply. "You make me feel things."

"What kinds of things?"

"Aargh. Just things, okay? Things I shouldn't feel."

Chloe squared her shoulders, her head tipped slightly up. "Why shouldn't you?"

"Because...you know already. We've gone over this before."

"We're not related," Chloe said.

"The boundaries." Ashton prompted.

"We'll cross them."

Ashton chuckled almost maniacally at Chloe's confidence. "No, Chloe. We won't." She abruptly stopped laughing and shook her head. "Even though I feel things doesn't mean I'll date you. I'm never going to date you. I wouldn't be able to stomach watching you go off with other people...with Trevor or Erin or whoever else you're dating. I don't want to be a part of that. That's not my world. That's your world and I don't belong in it."

"What if I you were the only person I saw?" Chloe challenged. "What if I dated you exclusively?"

"You would do that?"

Chloe gave pause, pursed her lips then answered. "Yeah. I would."

A dull ache throbbed against Ashton's temples. "No."

"Whaaat? Why the hell not?"

Ashton blinked back the oncoming teardrops threatening to break free from behind her long lashes. "I'm not going to have you change who you are and who you are is someone who specifically stated that they would never give their whole self to one person. Correct?"

"Yes, but I—"

"No! Stop," Ashton pleaded. "You be you and I'll be me and we'll just accept that we're incompatible. It wouldn't ever work out between us."

Chloe frowned. "There's definite compatibility here. I think we should at least try before calling it a wash. Don't you?"

"I feel like I've made it clear that I don't."

"Ashton, what else is this about?"

"What?"

"I'm picking up a vibe from you that there's more to you not wanting to date than our family stuff and our relationship preferences."

Ashton scoffed, nervously. "I hate to break it to you, but your vibe is defective."

Chloe sucked in a breath, her features sullen. "It's not though." She motioned to Ashton's left shoulder. "You don't completely trust me...is that it? A part of you believes I'll hurt you like she did."

Ashton stared silently at Chloe save for the soft sob that escaped her lungs.

Chloe nodded sorrowfully. "Okay...then what can I do to convince you that I won't?"

Ashton hastily toweled the wetness from her face with her hands and hugged herself. She exhaled a pained breath. "Nothing, so just be my friend like we agreed on. I won't avoid you. I swear. I'll be better. Alright?"

Chloe's eyes filled with emotion and she lowered her gaze. "Alright." She listlessly turned away from Ashton and shuffled towards the bedroom door. Before Ashton could find her voice to ask Chloe to stay, it was too late. Chloe was gone.

Chapter Fifteen

When Ashton awoke curled up in a ball on her bed, the sun had already set. Her pillow was damp with a fusion of tears and water from crying herself to sleep immediately after showering earlier. Disoriented, she uncoiled her body and eased herself into a seated position. She wiped away the still-wettish strands of hair that were plastered to her face and picked her phone off of the nightstand to check the time: 6:02 p.m. She read the missed text from Noah.

Yo! Family dinner is at seven tonight. I hope to see you there.

"Ugh." Ashton put the phone back on the table. She slowly got to her feet and made her way inside the bathroom. She frowned at her reflection. Her gray eyes were droopy and bloodshot. Her complexion was colorless. She pulled her long, dark brown locks to one side and tied them into a loose braid, securing it with the elastic she had been wearing around her wrist all day. She pinched her cheeks to give them pigmentation. She forced the corners of her mouth up into a smile, but it was useless. She kept staring at herself. "You have to follow through. You have to be the person you say you'll be. You can do this." She nodded, took the sweatshirt from the hook on the back of the door and slipped her arms through it. She zipped it all the way up, ensuring full coverage and headed for the bedroom's exit. As she passed the nightstand, she reclaimed her cell and crammed it inside the pocket of her hoodie. When Ashton reached the door, she squared her shoulders, exhaled and left for Chloe's room.

***

"It's open!" Chloe shouted in response to Ashton's knock at her bedroom door, her voice muffled by the wall's paneling.

Apprehensively, Ashton entered Chloe's room. She shut the door in her wake nearly noiselessly. Chloe sat cross-legged on her unmade bed. She looked up from the magazine in her hands, shook her head and sighed dejectedly.

"What?" Chloe asked.

Ashton took several hesitant steps in Chloe's direction and stopped only when her kneecaps bumped up against the side of Chloe's mattress. She glanced down at Chloe and when their eyes connected, Ashton ceased to breathe. For a moment, Ashton soaked in the seemingly flawless symmetry of Chloe's face. Upon recognizing that Chloe's deep brown irises were red-rimmed, Ashton's stomach sank.

"I'm sorry," Ashton said softly.

"Why for?"

"Making you upset."

Chloe shrugged. "I don't know what you're talking about. I'm fine." With her focus glued to Ashton, she blindly placed the magazine next to her. "Is that what you came to say?"

"No."

"Then why are you here?"

"I needed to tell you that I know you would never hurt me...like..." Ashton unconsciously ran her hand along her left arm and fell quiet.

"I'm glad you know that." Chloe scooched forward on the bed and uncrossed her legs, gingerly hooking them around either side of Ashton. She then reached up and took both of Ashton's hands in her own. Ashton's heartbeat pulsed in her ears as she found herself unable to resist or even move for that matter.

Chloe glimpsed at their attached bodies then her piercing stare met Ashton's. "Is this okay?"

The blood rushed to Ashton's head. Wooziness overcame her. "I...I, uh...okay."

"It's a promise." Chloe threaded her fingers between Ashton's. "I promise you, Ashton, I won't ever harm you."

Ashton gave a slow nod. "Alright."

Chloe smiled faintly at Ashton. "Why do you look so sad?"

"You haunt me. I can't escape you...not even in sleep." Ashton shook her head despairingly and disentangled her fingers from Chloe's.

"I'm sorry. I don't know what to—"

Ashton pressed her forefinger against Chloe's lips. A chill shot up Ashton's spine at the point of contact. Chloe sat perfectly still, gazing wide-eyed at Ashton.

"We shouldn't," Ashton whispered as she bent costively at the waist in a forward motion, her hand moving over to Chloe's warm cheek. When Ashton was close enough to taste Chloe's shallow exhale, Chloe shut her eyes. Chloe's hard swallow vibrated into Ashton's palm. "We shouldn't, but I..." Ashton gently brushed her lips across Chloe's. A desirous energy careened throughout Ashton. Chloe's mouth opened ever so slightly as she reached up and wrapped her arms around Ashton's neck. Ashton's parted lips smoothed over Chloe's again, this time with more fervor. The tip of Chloe's tongue grazed Ashton's, fueling the kiss. Ashton's head buzzed as their tongues touched; their mouths continuing to collide in harmony. Suddenly, Ashton gasped and pulled back haltingly, trying to catch her breath. "I'm so sorry."

"What?" Chloe rasped. "No. Why are you sorry? Don't be sorry."

"I. Uh. That was...inappropriate. I thought that if...I thought that if we kissed, it would help me get that–you–out of my system, and then we could resume our friendship, but I'm pretty sure I just made things worse for myself." Ashton went to stand up straight, but Chloe tightened her grip on Ashton.

"What are you saying?"

"Us being friends is not—"

"Girls!" Dean's voice boomed from downstairs. "Dinner's ready!"

Ashton closed her eyes and cursed under her breath. She looked at Chloe apologetically. "Never mind. Forget it. Please. Forget this ever happened." Ashton reached around her neck and unfastened Chloe's hold on her. Chloe stared at Ashton, confounded. "I really am sorry," Ashton mumbled once more as she turned and left Chloe's room.

Chapter Sixteen

"You kissed her?!" Katlyn exclaimed with wild eyes.

"Yes. That's what I said," Ashton spoke into the screen of her tablet.

"Omigod! Omigod! How was it? Don't leave out any detail."

"Dude...no."

"Why?"

"Kat, I'm so confused," Ashton bemoaned.

"Only you're not, buddy," Katlyn said. "You know exactly what you feel for her."

"I don't want to feel for her! These circumstances...this whole thing is just...messy. It's one big mess."

"And I don't want be all lovesick for a guy who thinks fantasy football is a real thing, but I am, so I deal. Dude, everybody feels things at times that they would rather not feel for one reason or another, but that's life, and yeah, life *is* messy. But it's life...you can't go around it because it's chaotic. You have to go through it. You have to live it," Katlyn said. "Embrace the chaos, my friend."

Ashton raised an eyebrow at Katlyn and sniffled. "Did you pull that from your library of self-help books?"

"No way, man. That came from my library of self-actualization books." Katlyn smirked. "Two different libraries."

Ashton chuckled. "I love you."

"I know."

"Tell me what to do."

Katlyn pouted. "I can't. Only you can do that."

"If you were me, what would you do?"

"That's kinda the same question."

"Kat, please."

"Aargh! You're a pain in my butt." Katlyn shook her head. "Alright. If I were you, I'd ask her to the concert like I thought we already agreed was the idea you were going to sit on anyways."

"She'll say no."

"You don't know what she'll say."

"Why would she even want to go with me? I kissed her and then left her there." Ashton palmed her forehead. "Then we didn't speak during dinner. We didn't look at each other. Nothing. Nada. Zip. It was incredibly awkward."

Katlyn nodded. "Well, in all fairness, *you're* incredibly awkward sometimes."

"Gee, thanks."

"Dude, just ask the girl to the concert. Tell her you're sorry for being a weirdo and then be like, 'hey, I have an extra ticket to this upcoming show. Wanna go?' Easy peasy."

Ashton scoffed. "Yeah, easy to say maybe. Not easy to do."

"It's never easy to do if it's worth it." Katlyn stared stringently at Ashton. "So you gotta ask yourself: do you want to remedy the status quo you have with Chloe? Is Chloe worth it?"

Ashton chewed on her thumbnail for a second before staring back at Katlyn. "Yes."

Katlyn grinned. "Atta girl! Now tell me about the kiss."

"Nope. Nice try though."

"Damn you."

Ashton sniggered. "You love me."

"I do, but I'll love you more if you *at least* tell me whether or not it what the best kiss you've ever had. I'm your best friend. I'm privy to this information. Those are the rules."

Ashton wrinkled her brow. "The best friend rules?"

"Um, yeah. Those would be them. Sooo...was your kiss with Chloe the best kiss you've ever had?"

"Mum's the word."

"Ha! Mum my ass! It totally was!"

***

Ashton lightly rapped her knuckles against Chloe's bedroom door and took a breath to brace herself. There was no answer. Ashton knocked again. A raging ball of nerves weighed heavily in the pit of her stomach. After several minutes, the door flung open and Chloe glowered at Ashton.

"What?" Chloe spewed.

Ashton swallowed. "I...uh." She dried her palms on her jeans. "May I come in?"

Chloe snorted. "No. you may not."

Ashton winced, her jaw slightly hanging loose. "Why not? I want to tell you something."

"Oh yeah?" Chloe slung the strap of her purse onto her right shoulder. "I feel like you said plenty earlier."

"No. About that. I...ugh. Please. Can we just talk?"

"Look, I'm sure whatever you have to say is riveting, but I've got somewhere to be and I don't have time to listen." Chloe paused and shook her head. "And I definitely don't have time to play games."

"I'm not playing games, Chloe."

"Psht. Then you certainly had me fooled." Chloe stepped outside of her room, closing the door behind her. The girls stood face to face. Ashton did not budge. "Move," Chloe ordered.

"Let me say my piece first."

"I don't know exactly which part of 'move' you don't comprehend so I'll try to be clearer." Chloe crossed her arms over her chest. "Get. Out. Of. My. Way." Her eyebrows lifted a little. "Understand?"

Ashton's heart plummeted from her chest. She mechanically placed her hand atop her left breast to alleviate the physical pain Chloe's callousness caused her. Ashton silently begged the universe to help keep her from crying. She choked back her tears. "I understand. You have to go but then can we talk later on tonight?"

Chloe's onyx eyes hardened even more. "I'm going out with Trevor. I have no idea when I'll be coming home. It's best for you to not wait."

"How about tomorrow? Can we talk tomorrow?"

A pinging sound echoed from Chloe's bag. "My ride's here. This is where you remove yourself from my path, which, to be honest, you're quite good at doing, and we go our separate ways."

"Is that a no?"

Chloe pressed her lips together and sneered. "Yahtzee."

"Wait."

"Uh. Uh. Nope. I'm tired of you fucking with my head."

"Chloe, I'm sorry. I wasn't trying to—"

"Aargh! Ashton, stop! We're done here."

With heavy feet, Ashton shifted to the side, giving Chloe space to pass by. Ashton kept her wet gaze on Chloe as she walked the length of the hall and made her way down the staircase. When the front door slammed shut, Ashton pressed her back against the wall, shut her eyes and began to cry.

Chapter Seventeen

"Ash, wake up." Noah's voice was an impatient whisper.

"Go away," Ashton grumbled, pulling the comforter up over her head.

"It's 10:02 in the morning. You never sleep this late."

"I was tired, alright?" Ashton spoke into her pillow.

"I thought you might be dead. Seriously."

Ashton groaned, rubbed her fatigued eyelids open and glared at Noah, who was hovering above her. "I assure you, I'm alive...and wide awake now thanks to you."

"Well, as your brother, it's my duty to worry about you."

"I appreciate your concern, but now that you know I have a working pulse, can you let me go back to sleep?"

"No way." Noah sat on the ledge of the bed. "Not until you tell me what your deal is? You're behaving unusually, and I'd like for you to tell me why that is."

"Really? You think I'm behaving unusually all because I slept in?"

"Um...yes. Yes I do."

"You're ridiculous."

"I'm your twin," Noah said. "I know you. Something's up. I feel it. So what is it?"

"Ugh. Can I at least have coffee running through my veins before we have a conversation?"

"No, but if you converse with me, I will buy you a gift card to The Bean."

Ashton raised an eyebrow. "You're bribing me? Really?"

"Is it working?"

"Depends. How much is said gift card gonna be worth?"

"Ten bucks."

"Lame."

Noah sighed. "Twenty-five dollars."

Ashton yawned. "I'm not feeling the whole talking right when I wake up thing."

"Oh my god. Fine. Fifty dollars."

"Okay. I'll bite," Ashton said. "I feel a little depressed. I miss Mom." She shrugged.

Noah frowned. "That's all?"

"Mmhmm."

"Then why were you crying last night outside of Chloe's bedroom?"

Ashton's mouth opened, horrified, as she threw the blankets off of her and vaulted out of bed, nearly knocking Noah over in the process. She pointed her finger at her brother. "What the fuck, Noah! You were spying on me?!"

Noah rubbed the back of his neck and winced. "Spying is such an eerie term. It's more like I happened to be leaving my room, *spotted* you and then snuck by you to go downstairs."

"Ha! Wow. So, not only were you snooping but you didn't even bother to console me?"

"You didn't exactly seem to be in an approachable condition, so I didn't approach you."

Ashton threw her hands in the air. "Oooh but you thought that now I'd be approachable?! That you could just wake me up and start grilling me? Asking me if something was wrong because you "felt" it when in actuality, you knew something was wrong because you bore witness to my being upset last night, you asshole!"

"Calm down."

"No. You don't get to tell me what to do." Ashton shook her head. "Go."

"Ash..."

"Leave, Noah."

"I don't care," Noah said quietly. "I won't judge you."

Ashton's eyes widened. "What are you talking about?"

"You were crying for her. For Chloe."

Ashton clenched her jaw and crossed her arms over her chest. "I tried..." She swallowed and a tear crawled down her cheek. "I tried not to have feelings for her. I did. And you told me that being interested in her was too close to home. The idea of it..." Ashton's voice cracked. "You were grossed out. I wanted to come to you but I was scared. I thought you'd disown me or something and I couldn't..."

Noah's hands were suddenly holding onto Ashton's shoulders. "Stop, okay?" He stared at her and took a breath. "Yes, I said those things because it's...different, but it's your life to live, not mine. And I don't want you to live a miserable life, which you'll end up doing if you're constantly lying to yourself and everyone else about who you really are and what you really want." Noah cleared his throat. "Ash, I love you no matter who have the feels for. You're my sister." He pulled Ashton closer into an embrace. Ashton wept against his chest.

"I don't know how to deal with this," Ashton blubbered. "I don't know what to do. I don't know where to go from here."

"Or maybe you do know and that's why you're an emotional train wreck."

Ashton slapped Noah's rib cage and glanced up at him. "I am not an emotional train wr—alright, I'm a little bit of a mess."

Noah smiled. "Yeah, you are."

"Please don't say anything."

"They might have a hard time with it and I might have said some stuff to make you worry about it, but I truly believe that they're not going to ridicule you or desert you or—"

"Noah. Please. Do not say anything. We can't be sure how they'll react."

"Okay. Your secret's safe."

"Thank you." Ashton sniffled. "Besides, there isn't much to tell."

Noah's brow wrinkled. "What's that supposed to mean?"

"She isn't interested...not anymore."

"Huh." Noah nodded. "That's what she told you?"

"Um. Well...er...no, but—"

"But nothing, dummy. Pull yourself together, be a badass lesbian, and go get the girl."

***

Once showered and dressed, Ashton found herself at the top of the staircase staring at the landing. The foyer reverberated with familiar voices...including

Chloe's. Ashton's heart began pounding against her chest at an alarming speed. Her throat thickened and she swallowed back a mouthful of dry air. She coughed, inhaled sharply and grabbed the railing with a shaky grip. Weak-kneed, Ashton slowly made her way down the steps. When she reached the landing, she eyed the stairs and briefly considered skulking back up them. "You got this," she whispered to herself. She straightened her posture and strolled through the dining room, towards the kitchen, where all the sound was originating from. Noah was seated on one side of the bar, making grand hand gestures as he spoke to Chloe, who stood opposite Noah, her backside facing Ashton. As he finished speaking, Noah slapped the countertop and Chloe laughed. The sonorous noise stirred Ashton's insides.

Mid-chuckle, Noah raised his eyes to Chloe and espied Ashton standing next to the kitchen table. Ashton nervously hooked her thumbs in the front pockets of her jeans and smiled weakly at her brother. Noah cleared his throat and glanced at the watch on his left wrist.

"I should get going. I'm meeting Lily for brunch," Noah said.

Chloe nodded. "Ah. Very cool. Have a good time."

"Thank you. I intend to." Noah got up and started in Ashton's direction. "Ash! Fancy bumping into you here."

Ashton cringed and shook her head as Chloe slowly turned around to face Noah and Ashton.

"Um. Yeah. Totally fancy," Ashton said. "Where are you off to?"

"I have plans with my lady friend."

"I see." Ashton pressed her lips into a tight smile. "Well, enjoy then."

"I will." Noah grinned. "You do the same with your day." His eyes widened. "You feel me?"

Ashton's brow furrowed, silently beseeching her brother to stop talking. "Nope. I do not. Good talk though. You should go now. Don't want to be late." She clutched Noah's bicep and gave him a small pull in the direction of the exit. "Buh bye."

"Psht. Rude." Noah smoothed his hand over his wrinkled shirt sleeve when Ashton released him. "If that's how it's gonna be then I'll be on my way." He lifted his right palm in a quasi-wave. "Later," Noah said coolly and strutted out of the kitchen. "Don't forget what we chatted about, Ash!" He called after himself before the sound of the front door closing rang throughout the house.

Ashton internally winced and looked shrinkingly over at Chloe. "Hey."

Chloe made a motion with her head towards the exit. "What was that about?"

Panic engulfed Ashton. "Huh?" She swallowed. "What was what about?"

"You show up and suddenly your brother has to bolt but not without communicating with you in some strange twin code first. So I'll ask you again: what was that about?"

"Do you really want to hear the answer?"

Chloe rolled her eyes. "No. I'm asking you for kicks. Yes. I want the answer."

"Then does this mean we're on speaking terms again?"

"Aargh!"

"Alright, alright." Ashton exhaled a trembling breath. "It was about you."

"Oh. Okay." Chloe pursed her lips. "So now you're talking about me behind my back. Awesome."

"No. It's not like that."

"Then what's it like, Ashton?"

"I told Noah that I..." Ashton pinched the rogue, dark brown curl that had fallen from her French braid onto her forehead between her index finger and thumb and tucked it behind her right ear. "That I...um." She half-chuckled at her own nervousness. With a faux sense of aloofness, Ashton brought her gaze to Chloe's face. The moment their stares came together, Ashton's heart skipped. She gulped. "I told Noah that I had feelings for you."

Chloe nodded, folded her arms over her chest and leaned back against the bar. "Yeah? And did you tell him what a spectacular job you do repressing those feelings?"

"Not exactly, but sort of."

"Why would you do that?"

"Do what?"

"Share that with Noah," Chloe said.

"Because having this massive crush on you and constantly trying to pretend it doesn't exist is exhausting and it's making me miserable. I don't want to be miserable."

"What *do* you want then?"

Ashton's throat thickened with uneasiness. She swallowed forcibly, and nodded slowly as she readied herself to answer Chloe's question. She lifted her eyes up to fall in with Chloe's rich, brown irises. Ashton's breath suddenly seized in the cavity of her clenched chest. She let out a short cough to clear her airway. "Uh. To...um...to date. You." Ashton scratched her bottom lip with her top teeth. "For us to date."

Chloe's eyebrows narrowed suspiciously as she stared bemusedly at Ashton. "I'm sorry. Did you say you wanted to date me?"

Ashton raised her chin to appear confident. "Yes. That is what I said."

"Huh. I see. And what happened to all of your convictions about why we can't be together?"

"They're gone."

"Mmm. They just...disappeared?"

"Not quite." Ashton shrugged. "I realized I was being stubborn and scared."

Chloe gave Ashton a sad, half-smile. "Look, Ashton. I'm glad that you had some sort of awakening or whatever and that now you know what you want, but I think you were right before. I think it's best if we're only friends."

Ashton gaped. "What? Why? Did your feelings change?"

"No. Not even a little, but that's just it: I'm sure about what I want. I've never wavered and you...well, you're very...uh...back and forth." Chloe frowned. "You already messed around with my emotions once and it sucked. Who's to say you won't change your mind? I don't need that kind of drama in my life."

"I apologize for what I did." Ashton exhaled. "Chloe, I'm sure now. Really, I am."

Chloe blinked back a frustrated tear. "I appreciate your apology. Thank you. And I'll be your friend, but nothing more."

"Why not?"

"It's safer."

"Safer how?"

"It's pretty clear."

"Not to me, it isn't. How is safer?" Ashton asked.

"It just is, alright?"

"Chloe, no. It's not alright. Talk to me. Is this about you being polyamorous because I've mentally prepared myself to be part of your...er...rotation."

Chloe's dark eyes widened and she scoffed. "My rotation? Seriously?!"

Ashton winced. "I'm sorry. I don't know how...I was trying not to offend you."

"You were unsuccessful. I'm offended."

"I'm sorry. Tell me how to make it better."

"For starters, you could listen to me when I speak."

Ashton's forehead creased. "What?"

"Aargh! I've said this before but apparently you need me to say it again: If I ever were to date you, I'd date you exclusively."

"And I told you before that I don't want you to change the way you are to appease me."

"It's not about 'appeasing' you. It's about me and what I want–wanted–with you." Chloe shook her head. "Did the idea ever occur to you that maybe I think you're...an exception? Like maybe I feel different around you than I do around other people and maybe I want–wanted–to explore that. Just the two of us; without the distraction of having several individuals involved. What I do with my relationships and what I want out of them is my call to make. My life. My choice. Get it?"

"Yes," Ashton mumbled.

"Good."

"Soo, there *is* a possibility that you would date me?"

"Ashton!"

Ashton held up her hands. "Okay. Okay."

The girls stared at one another in a long moment of silence until Ashton finally spoke. "Really though. Would you date me?"

A low growl escaped Chloe. "*Did* I want to date you? Yes. You know I did. That was then. But after everything that's gone down between us what with my mind being fucked with and you obviously not trusting that I won't hurt you the way your ex did, I don't think it would be wise of us to pursue anything other than a friendship. It wouldn't be safe. Is *that* clear enough for you?" She quickly wiped away the wetness from her left cheek.

Ashton dropped her gaze to the floor and stifled a sob. "Yeah. It's clear."

"Besides, you're leaving in a few weeks and—"

"Stop." Ashton glared at Chloe. "You made your point."

Chloe nodded.

Ashton turned and began to walk away.

"Ashton, wait!" Chloe's voice echoed throughout the kitchen.

Ashton glanced over her shoulder at Chloe. "What?"

"If you're up for it, we could hang out sometime soon...like as friends."

"Yeah. Sure," Ashton said apathetically and disappeared from Chloe's sight.

Chapter Eighteen

"That's it? You just walked away?" Noah stared at Ashton, wild-eyed and perplexed.

"Yes. That's what happened. I walked away," Ashton said. "What the hell else was I supposed to do?"

"You could have been more persistent."

"Dude, you weren't there. She was adamant about not dating me. I can't force her to give me a chance. So, no. I wasn't going to persist."

"Shit. I didn't see that coming." Noah shook his head. "I thought she'd be all about dating you after what you told me."

Ashton sighed. "I feel like I should've known it wasn't going to be that simple. I pushed her away. She has every right to be upset. Also, your advice fucking blows, bro. It always has. That's a lesson I totally should have learned by now."

Noah gasped. "Untrue. I command you to take that back. I give damn good advice. I'm a wise man."

"Ha!"

"Well if my advice is so bad, why do you continue to come to me for my input? Huh? Huh? Huh? What do you have to say to that?"

Ashton rolled her eyes. "Don't be an asshole." She leaned against Noah's bedroom wall and groaned. "I come to you because you're the only person I have to go to."

"You know that's bogus. You have Kat."

"Yes, but Kat but gets me in a different way than you do."

"The twin thing?"

Ashton nodded. "Exactly. The twin thing."

"I understand."

"Thank you."

"Alright. What's your next move then?" Noah asked.

Ashton gunned a look of disbelief at her brother. "For real?! Did you even hear what I told you?"

"I heard you. Chloe rejected you and you dipped."

"Wow. Way to summarize."

"That's basically the gist of it. Is it not?"

Ashton sneered.

"Well?" Noah pressed.

Ashton exhaled dispiritedly and pouted. "Yeah. I guess it is."

Noah stepped closer to Ashton and placed his hands on her shoulders. "Ash, you gave up way too easy. You need a new game plan."

"Ugh. No. That's not what I need. She flat out stated that she didn't want to date me. I have to respect that."

"That's fair, but you still gotta do something. You have to *show* her that she's important to you. You feel me?"

"I feel you."

"Coolness." Noah tilted his head to the side. "Now you said that the way things left off was that she told you she would hang out with you. Yes?"

"Yes."

Noah grinned. "I have a suggestion."

Ashton pursed her lips. "Go on."

"Do you really want to know? Because I've been told that my advice blows."

"Jesus," Ashton muttered. "Okay. I'm sorry I said that. Please tell me what your suggestion is."

"Ask her to go somewhere with you tonight after dinner."

"Tonight? Are you nuts? That doesn't give either of us time to recover from the conversation we had earlier."

"There's nothing to recover from. Stop being so emo."

Ashton stuck her tongue out at Noah.

"Because *that's* mature."

"Aargh." Ashton took a deep breath. "You want me to just approach her, act as if everything's fine and ask her to hang out with me? Tonight?"

"Yup."

"And if she rejects me again?"

"She won't."

"How are you certain?"

"She'll be impressed by your perseverance," Noah said. "But remember that this is your chance to let her know that you're in it to win it."

Ashton quirked an eyebrow. "In it to win it? Dude, nobody says that."

"Well, I just did. Now get outta here." Noah squeezed Ashton's shoulders before releasing her from his grip. "You can do this."

Ashton gave her brother a small, unsure smile. "Uh huh." She stepped towards the door of Noah's room and paused once her hand wrapped around the doorknob. "This isn't going to work."

"It will. Have faith."

***

Ashton traipsed down the hallway to Chloe's room. She kept her eyes fixed on the door as she wiped her sweaty palms across the back of jeans. When Ashton reached her destination, she held onto the doorframe with her left hand, bracing herself. She knocked softly. It remained quiet on the other side of the door. She knocked again and listened intently. Nothing.

"She went out for the night." Dean spoke in a low, calm tone as he made his way up the stairs behind Ashton.

Startled by the unexpected presence of her father, Ashton spun around. "What?"

Dean smiled softly. "Sorry. I didn't mean to scare you. I was just letting you know that if you're looking for Chloe, she went out for the night."

Ashton's insides twisted and the corners of her mouth unconsciously turned down. "Oh."

"Is everything okay?"

"Yeah. Everything's fine."

Dean nodded. "Alright. Good. Just thought I'd ask because neither of you said much during dinner earlier."

"Wasn't much to say."

"Uh huh." Dean rubbed the short stubble on this cheek thoughtfully. "Well, what are your plans for this evening?"

Ashton's eyes widened. "My plans? Um. I was...er...there's a movie. Yes. That's it. I was going to stream a movie online."

"I don't suppose you'd consider postponing your movie to have a drink with your old man."

"A drink? Like with alcohol?"

Dean chuckled. "No. I was thinking more along the lines of hot cocoa."

"Right. Of course."

"So? How 'bout that drink?"

Ashton dug the toe of her right sneaker into the carpet and moved it back and forth. "Dean, I appreciate the offer, but—"

"We have mini marshmallows," Dean practically sang. "Do you still take six?"

Ashton flinched. "You remember that?"

"Absolutely, I remember!" He laughed. "You were insistent. It *had* to be six. No more and no less. That's the only way you'd drink it." His laughter died down and his smile softened. "Ashton, you're my daughter. I couldn't possibly forget. I would never want to forget. I love you and your brother."

Ashton quickly averted her eyes away from her father. She stared at the dent her foot had created in the rug. "I guess if you have six marshmallows to spare, I could make time for hot cocoa."

Dean grinned. "Wonderful!"

***

Ashton sat opposite Dean on a tall stool at the kitchen counter. She used her spoon to continuously stir the marshmallows floating atop her cup of hot cocoa.

"I heard a rumor that drinks actually taste better if you drink them," Dean said.

Ashton blinked and looked up at her father. She pressed her lips into a tight smile. "Sorry. My mind was wandering."

Dean took a sip of his beverage. "Do you want to talk to your old man about it?"

"About what?"

"About whatever is on your mind."

Ashton shook her head and lifted her cup to her mouth. "No," she mumbled before taking a drink. She glanced around the otherwise vacant kitchen. "Where's Regina?"

"She's upstairs reading to Ariel to put her to sleep."

Ashton nodded. "Should I read to her tomorrow night when I babysit?"

"If you want to. That's up to you."

"Cool."

"She's a good baby," Dean said. "She has a good temperament. She reminds me of how Noah was as an infant."

Ashton's forehead wrinkled. "Psht. Noah? What about me?"

Mr. Daniels snorted. "Are you joking? You were fussing all the time when you were a baby. You drove your mother and me bonkers."

Ashton sniggered. "Bonkers?"

"Are you making fun of me?"

"I think it's safe to say that. Yeah." Ashton tasted more of her hot cocoa.

Dean's expression lightened. He cleared his throat. "Thanks for agreeing to have a drink with me. I'm enjoying this."

Ashton swallowed the marshmallow she had been chewing. "Well, don't get used to it. I just happened to be feeling charitable this evening, so you lucked out."

"Right." Dean pursed his lips. "I understand."

"Good."

"Tell me then, since we might not get to do this again, have you made any new friends here? I never really see you go out."

"No. Why bother? It's July. I leave at the end of next month."

"It's nice to make connections whenever you can, wherever you are. You could still keep in touch once you're back in Florida."

"Nah. I'll pass. I'm content with the friends I have now."

"Okay. What about girls?"

Ashton coughed on the hot cocoa that was making its way down her throat. Dean stood up, but Ashton raised her palm, silently stopping him from coming to her aid. After a few seconds of hacking, she calmly took a napkin from the dispenser at the end of the counter and wiped her mouth.

"Are you alright?" Dean asked.

"Fabulous," Ashton grumbled.

"Are you being sarcastic?"

Ashton glared at her father. "What do you think, Dean? Yes. I'm being sarcastic. Why the hell are you asking me about girls?"

"Because you're my child and I want to know more about what's going on in your life and if you're dating and you're gay."

Ashton make-believed gasped. "I'm gay?"

Mr. Daniels rolled his eyes. "I'm sorry. That's not what I meant. I just meant that I know you're gay and I was trying to ask you if there's anyone you're interested in. Romantically. So I brought up girls."

"Yeah. You sure did."

"It was supposed to sound casual."

"Only it didn't."

"I realize that." Dean frowned. "May I try again?"

"Ha! Seriously? You want to talk about girls with me? Nope."

"Why not? Noah discusses his dating life with me and so does Chloe."

Ashton's heartbeat momentarily lapsed. "She does...er...um...they do?"

"Yes. Not in detail but they let me in a little."

"Huh." Ashton nodded. "Good for them, but I'm not going to talk about that sort of stuff with you. If you want to try to start a dialogue with me again, I can't stop you but the topic of dating is off limits."

Mr. Daniels exhaled. "Okay. I'll remember that." He emptied the remnants of his cup into his mouth. "That was some quality cocoa. Don't you think?"

Ashton arched an eyebrow. "Mmm. The best," she said unenthusiastically.

"Alright. Let me try a different approach." Dean smiled. "Are you looking forward to college? Your mother told me you'll be attending Rose University this fall."

"What you heard is true. I am going to Rose and I'm excited. What else you got?"

Dean rested his hands on the counter and folded them together. "Your mother also told me that you got accepted to Miranda University here in Massachusetts."

"I did. What of it?"

"Miranda has a better nursing program."

Ashton grit her teeth. "How did you know I wanted to study nursing?"

"Your mother told me."

"Of course she did."

"Please don't be upset with her. I would be completely in the dark about anything having to do with you and Noah if not for her."

Ashton silently shook her head.

"I'm curious as to why you chose to pass up a great opportunity here and stay in Florida instead," Dean said.

"I like the palm trees."

"Uh huh. That's all you're going to give me, isn't it?"

"Yup."

"Ashton, I just want you and your brother to be happy. When it comes down to it, I don't care where you choose to live or study or who you love, so long as you're happy. Do you hear what I'm saying?"

"Yes."

"And I really want to be a part of your and your brother's worlds. You guys are my kids."

Ashton got to her feet. "How do I know you won't leave my world again if I were ever to invite you in?"

"I can promise you that I won't."

"Coming from you, Dean, that's weak."

"Then give me a chance to prove to you that I can be true to my word."

"And why would I do that?" Ashton asked.

"Haven't you ever wanted someone to give you a second chance?"

An image of Chloe immediately flashed before Ashton. She threw her head back. "Aargh!" Ashton slowly leveled her face with her father's and glowered at him. "Fine. I'll give you your second chance, but let it be known that I'm doing this for mom and for Noah because *they* asked me to...not because you're asking me to. And if you hurt me or Noah anymore than you already have, we are so done. Got it?"

Dean smiled broadly. "Got it." He slid off of the stool and rounded the counter towards Ashton.

Ashton held up her index finger. "We're not hugging so get that out of your head now."

Mr. Daniels nodded and stuck his hand out.

"Jesus," Ashton whispered and shook her father's hand. After a moment, she loosened her grip and let her arm fall to her side. "Goodnight, Dean," Ashton said and started for her room.

Chapter Nineteen

Ashton crept through the entrance of her father's house around half-past seven Friday morning after her jog. To her surprise, there was a stillness to all the rooms on the first floor even though the sprinkling of the shower upstairs was audible. She let out a breath of relief; her muscles relaxing along with the exhale.

"What's with the stealthy act you got going on every time you come through that door?"

At the sound of Chloe's voice, Ashton's heart ricocheted against her clenched chest. She quickly looked to her left. The dining room was dark, but the rising sun seeping through the shades cast enough light inside so that Ashton could make out a little more than just Chloe's silhouette. She was sitting in the chair closest to the edge of the table nursing a mug of coffee, sporting a pair of oversized, black sweatpants and a tight, white camisole. Her blonde hair was slightly disheveled, her complexion hadn't yet been touched by make-up and her brilliant, brown stare concentrated on Ashton and Ashton alone. Ashton stood, spellbound by Chloe's allure.

When it finally registered that Chloe was waiting for Ashton to answer her question, Ashton found her vocal chords. "Um. I...uh. I'm always worried I'll disturb someone if I'm too loud or something."

Chloe shrugged with her mouth. "It's a busy household. I wouldn't worry about it. However, one might think you were continuing with your avoidant behavior."

Ashton pursed her lips. "That's reasonable." She paused for a moment. "One might not be that far off in such thinking." She partially simpered at

Chloe and her belly flipped when Chloe reciprocated with a half-smile of her own.

Ashton rubbed the back of her neck, cleared her throat, and took several tentative steps towards the dining room without taking her eyes off her sneakers. When she reached the long, wooden table, she grabbed onto the edge with both hands and leaned the slightest bit forward. Surreptitiously, she inhaled Chloe's faint, floral scent blended with nutty aroma of fresh brewed coffee. Ashton's pulse thrummed in her ears. She swallowed, lifted her head and finally turned her gaze to meet Chloe's.

"You weren't home after dinner last night," Ashton remarked.

Chloe smirked a little. "Nope. I was not, but what's it to you?"

"I was looking for you."

"Is that so?"

Ashton nodded. "It is...so."

"What for?"

"Were you out with Erin?" Ashton asked meekly.

"No."

"Trevor?"

Chloe sighed. "Ashton, why does it matter to you who I was out with? Can't you just tell me why you were looking for me?"

"Because I—" Ashton shut her eyes tightly and shook her head.

"Because you what?"

After a long moment, Ashton stared at Chloe. She chewed on her bottom lip for a second. "Because I wanted to ask you if you'd hang out with me, but you...you weren't there."

Chloe searched Ashton's expression. "And what about now?"

The crease between Ashton's eyebrows deepened. "What about now?"

"Well, you said you *wanted* to ask me...as in the past tense." Chloe took a sip of her coffee. "Sooo, I'm asking you what you want now...in the present."

"I. Umm. I..."

Chloe placed her right hand over Ashton's and both girls instantly froze, their eyes locked on one another. Chloe inhaled sharply through her nose. "How's this: if you ask me, I promise I won't say no." She flashed Ashton a small smile.

A light shade of crimson tinged Ashton's cheeks and she smiled back at Chloe. "Do you want to hang out with me today?"

"Yes. Yes, I do."

"Cool."

"What do you want to do?" Chloe asked.

"Huh?"

Chloe chuckled. "Customarily, when a person asks another person to hang out, they have something in mind, like a place they want to go to or an activity they want to do. See where I'm going with this?"

Ashton's blush intensified. "I didn't actually think that far in advance, but in my defense, it wouldn't have made a difference anyways because I'm not familiar with what there is to do and see around here. I'm in foreign territory. Therefore, it's only logical that you pick what we should do."

Chloe raised a brow at Ashton. "Wow. You really are the daughter of a lawyer."

Ashton stuck her tongue out at Chloe. "Whatever."

"Alright. I have an idea."

"What is it?"

"I'm not telling."

Ashton gaped. "How come?"

"To keep you in suspense."

"I don't like being in suspense."

Chloe laughed. "Yeah. I'm getting that."

"Then you'll tell me?"

"Ha! No. Just trust me. Can you do that?"

"Ugh! Fine."

"Good," Chloe said with a grin. "We need to get a move on then because I have plans later."

Ashton's gut knotted. "Right. For your date."

"Yup."

"That works cuz I have babysitting duties tonight anyhow."

"Okay then. Nice. Meet me back here in an hour at nine."

Ashton pouted. "That doesn't give me a whole lot of time to shower and change my clothes."

Chloe's eyes unhurriedly roamed over Ashton's physique, adorned in snug running pants cropped right below the knees and an equally close-fitting lightweight tank top. She licked her lips. "No one said you had to change."

Ashton folded her arms across her chest. "Uh. Yeah. So I'm going upstairs to get ready now. I'll be here at nine."

"Mmm hmm. I will most definitely see you then."

***

As the wheels of the SUV crackled over the gravel, Chloe turned the stereo down and came to a slow stop. "Here we are!" She put the vehicle in park, unfastened her seatbelt, and turned to Ashton, who quietly sat in the passenger seat. Chloe gave Ashton a lopsided grin. The summer sun bouncing off the windshield magnified the darkness of her twinkling, brown eyes. Immediately, Ashton began to suffer from a shortness of breath as her pulse raced. With all the air trapped in her lungs, Ashton fought to remain poker-faced. She nodded and glanced out the window to free herself from Chloe's excruciatingly beautiful stare.

"Is something the matter?" Chloe asked.

Ashton shook her head, plastered a smile on her face and looked at Chloe. "No. It's perfect."

"It is. And I know I already brought you here, but in my opinion, this reservation is better than any popular tourist attraction there is." Chloe abruptly frowned. "Fuck. Did you want to see a popular tourist attraction? Because I could take you sightseeing instead if that's really what you—"

Ashton instinctually placed her forefinger over Chloe's lips. "Shh. I said this is perfect." Chloe fell silent. Everything fell silent. The spacious vehicle suddenly became very cramped as Chloe and Ashton's gazes bore into one another's. Heedfully, Ashton lifted her finger from Chloe's mouth and lowered her hand. "Sorry. I'm sorry."

Chloe cleared her throat. "Right. So as I was saying, it's way chill here what with the whole tranquil thing going on and such. I was thinking we could sit by the water and just talk...or whatever."

"Yeah. Totally." Ashton snapped off her seatbelt and got out of the SUV. She stared up at the treetops and let the fresh air fill her lungs with much needed oxygen. She shut her eyes tight for a second then turned around in the direction of Chloe's footsteps shuffling over the crushed rock beneath them as she came closer to where Ashton stood.

"Shall we?" Chloe nodded towards the stone bench near the water.

"Mmm hmm." Ashton started towards the seat with Chloe at her heels. When she reached the bench, Ashton eased herself down onto it. She rested her forearms on her legs, folded her hands together, and leaned forward. She stared ahead at the water. When Chloe sat down beside her, Ashton's skin covered in goose bumps. She shivered.

"You cold?" Chloe asked.

"What?"

"Are you cold? You just shivered."

"No. I'm good."

"You sure? I have a blanket in the trunk somewhere. I can get it."

"No, really. I'm good," Ashton said. "Thank you though."

"Okay."

A slight breeze caused a small ripple in the water and a few tree branched swayed. Ashton caught a whiff of Chloe's perfume and it became all that Ashton could smell. The aroma made her swimmy.

"What are you thinking about?" Chloe asked.

"Nothing. I'm just taking it in."

"Taking what in?"

The smell of you. "The view," Ashton replied dishonestly. "I'm enjoying how picturesque this fresh water lake looks." She glanced at Chloe through her peripheral. "You know it's one of two fresh water lakes in this seven hundred acre reservation."

Chloe giggled. "Wow. You're blatantly making fun of me. You're packing some serious spunk there, aren't you?"

Ashton gasped. "Make fun of you? Me? Never. I remembered the facts you gave me. That's all."

"You're fibbing."

"I fib not."

"Riiight. You're going to sit here and tell me you weren't making fun of me?"

"Affirmative."

"Fibber!"

"Am not."

"Then look at me and tell me you weren't making fun of me," Chloe demanded.

"Are you trying to test me?"

"Oh. You bet your sweet ass I'm testing you."

"So you think my ass is sweet?" Ashton half-grinned.

"Actually, yes, I do." Chloe cleared her throat. "But that's beside the point. Now look at me and let's see if you can fib to my face."

Don't make eye contact. You'll want to kiss her and she only wants to be friends. Ashton held up her hands while she kept her focus on the river. "Alright. I forfeit." Ashton nodded. "You win. I *was* making fun of you. I'm sorry."

Chloe chuckled. "You don't have to be sorry, but you *will* have to look at me eventually."

Ashton's body tensed. She said nothing.

"I'm not dense," Chloe said. "What's up with the no eye contact routine?"

Ashton shook her head then turned her gaze to Chloe. The second their eyes connected, desire surged through Ashton. The thudding of her heart against her chest became erratic and relentless. She slowly exhaled. "There. I'm looking at you. Happy?"

"Yep!" Chloe beamed. "So, I ran into Dean this morning while you were showering and he was all chipper and shit. Whistling and that sort of nonsense and I got to thinking that maybe last night he and my mom—"

"Whoa! Hey! Hey! Hey! Please for the love of god, do not finish that sentence."

Chloe laughed. "That's not where I was going with my story. Relax." She paused thoughtfully then her face contorted. "Eww. Now I have a grotesque mental image. Thanks."

Ashton sniggered. "It can't be any worse than the one I've got." Her top lip curled in disgust. "Alright. Where was your story going then?"

"Well." Chloe crossed her right leg over her left. "We greeted one another and he randomly jumped into this whole narration about how he got to hang out with you yesterday evening...and that there was even cocoa involved. True or false?"

"True."

Chloe smiled. "The man was on frickin' cloud nine."

Ashton shrugged. "I don't know why. There wasn't much to it. Small talk and a beverage."

"With *you* though." Chloe's eyes widened. "Ashton, your dad wanted so much for just a little of your time to bond or whatever and it finally happened. That's big."

"It's nothing."

"You're wrong."

"No. I'm not. You're blowing this way out of proportion."

Chloe rolled her eyes. "I beg to differ, but I won't fight with you about it. Just know that it meant a lot to him and I think it's rad that you gave him a chance."

"Well if you and Noah hadn't been up my ass about it on the regular than I probably wouldn't have. And I guess it finally dawned on me that we're all only human. As humans, we fuck up. *I* fuck up. Honestly, I wouldn't–I don't– ever want my mistakes held against me for the rest of my life. I'd want to be forgiven." Ashton sucked in a breath. "But how can I expect to be forgiven if I'm not willing to forgive? That's not exactly fair."

Chloe gave Ashton a lopsided smile. "How enlightened of you."

"Oh yeah. It must be something in the smoggy Boston air."

"Hey now! No need to go dissing our air." Chloe let out a small laugh then playfully bumped her shoulder into Ashton's. "I'm proud of you...for talking to your dad."

"Right. So enough about me. Spotlight's on you now." Ashton stuck her tongue out at Chloe.

"Ahh. Okay. I can take a hint. Shoot."

Ashton sized up Chloe and pursed her lips. "Alright. I got one." She motioned to Chloe's neck. "That necklace you're wearing."

Chloe raised an eyebrow. "What about it?"

"You wear it every day. Why?"

Chloe smirked. "So is this you confessing that you check me out every day?"

Ashton flushed. "I...no. I'm just...I see it on you. A lot."

"Mmhmm. Suuure. Well, that's because you're right: I do wear it every day."

"What is it a design of?"

"It's the Celtic Trinity Knot."

"What does it represent?"

"Geez. Inquisitive much?"

Ashton bowed her head a little. "Sorry."

"Relax, woman. I was only teasing you." Chloe fingered the pendant hanging from her neck. "It can represent lots of things. It really depends on how the person wearing it chooses to interpret it."

Ashton bit her bottom lip, partially wincing. "I have another question."

"I'm shocked." Chloe deadpanned.

Ashton frowned, but Chloe broke into a smile and spoke. "I'm only messing with you, Ashton. What's your question?"

"Alright then. What does it represent to you?" Ashton asked quietly.

"To me, it symbolizes the unity of the mind, body, and spirit."

Ashton nodded. "Huh. That's deep."

"Not really, but wearing it helps remind me to be my authentic, whole self, always."

Ashton smiled softly. "Thanks for sharing."

"You're welcome."

"I used to think I was good at being who I am but she...Felicia...it wasn't ever enough for her." Ashton looked to the water. "I tried though, but..."

"Shh."

Ashton did not flinch when Chloe's hand gently cupped her right cheek. She did not move away when Chloe's thumb erased the tear streaking Ashton's face. Ashton went to turn her head towards Chloe but Chloe was close. Close enough to kiss. And Chloe only wants to be friends. Ashton shut her eyes. Her body absorbed Chloe's touch. In the same breath, Ashton's desire shook her bones and cracked her racing heart, leaving a bittersweet taste in her mouth.

"You are enough," Chloe whispered.

Ashton got up quickly and took a few steps closer to the water's edge. She rubbed her eyes dry. "Wow. Sorry about that."

"You don't have to apologize." Chloe's voice was slightly distant. She was still on the bench.

"Anyways, how do you feel about dubstep violin?"

Chloe chuckled. "Um. That was random."

"This is me trying to change the subject."

"Yeah. I got that. You know, because of the subtlety you don't have."

Ashton crooked her head to face Chloe. "Har har."

Chloe grinned.

"Well? Where are you on dubstep violin?" Ashton persisted.

"I'm into it."

"Cool cuz I happen to have an extra ticket to the Eliza Diamonds concert. It's next month."

"Do you now?"

Ashton walked back to Chloe and stood in front of her. She turned her gaze downwards to meet Chloe's eyes. "I do."

"I'm not going to make this easy for you." Chloe pursed her lips. "You're going to have to ask me. So I'm gonna sit right here and wait for the question."

Ashton gasped. "But I basically did ask."

"True, but you need to legit ask me, and I realize this is difficult for you, which is why I'm making you do it. You need to conquer some of your fears. So, essentially, I'm doing you a favor." Chloe winked at Ashton.

Ashton snarled.

"Charming," Chloe said. "You're off to a great start."

"Ugh!" Ashton shook her head. "Okay. I can do this."

"You can totally do this."

Ashton cleared her throat. "Chloe, will you...do you maybe...would you like to go to the concert with me?"

Chloe smiled faintly and stood. Instinctively, Ashton stopped breathing.

"I would love to," Chloe said. "Now will you do something for me?"

"Uh. Yeah. Sure. What?"

Chloe reached around her own neck with both of her hands and unclasped her necklace. She carefully removed it and took Ashton's left hand. She placed the pendant in Ashton's palm. "Keep this safe for me."

Emotion nearly choked Ashton. "I will," she murmured.

"Thank you." Chloe leaned in and her lips barely grazed Ashton's forehead. "Hey, I think it's time."

Ashton's stomach tumbled. "Time for what?" Her voice was low.

"Time to hit the road or we'll both be late for our evening plans."

The crack in Ashton's heart grew larger. "Right. Let's go."

Chapter Twenty

"We really appreciate this," Dean said to Ashton as he tucked his wallet into the back pocket of his slacks.

"Yes. We really do." Regina fished through the purse hanging from her shoulder and pulled a twenty-dollar bill from it. She handed the money to Ashton. "Use this to order something for dinner."

Ashton accepted the money. "Thank you."

"There are take-out menus in the junk drawer next to the utensil drawer," Dean explained.

Ashton glanced towards the kitchen. "Gotcha."

"Each of our cell numbers are on the refrigerator," Regina said. "We'll both have our phones on."

Ashton nodded. "Okay."

"And the name and number of the restaurant is there too," Dean said.

"Good to know."

Regina bent down on one knee next to Ariel, who was half-sitting up in her cushioned, portable rocker. She smoothed her hand over the baby's head, planted a kiss on the child's cheek, and stood up again. Regina smiled at Ashton. "She's very well-behaved."

"Yeah. Dean mentioned that."

"She's already had her dinner and her diaper's been changed," Regina said. "All you need to do is lay her in the crib around eight o' clock and she should fall asleep fairly quickly."

"Alright."

"Please make sure the baby monitor is on in her room and that you have the parent unit near you at all times." Dean pointed to the cordless phone-looking device on the kitchen counter.

"Will do," Ashton said.

"Any questions?" Regina queried.

Ashton shook her head. "Nope."

The jangling of keys caused Ashton to look to the staircase, where Chloe was making her way down the steps. She reached the landing, met Ashton's eyes and gave her a nod of recognition. Ashton returned the gesture. Chloe then began to waltz over to Regina and Dean. She smiled widely at them. "I'm outie." She pecked them each on the cheek. "Enjoy your Indian feast."

"Thank you," Regina said. "Don't forget to be home by curfew."

"Yes, Mother."

"Be safe and have fun," Dean said to Chloe.

"You got it." Chloe turned her focus on Ashton and her smile evaporated. "Have a good night, you." She took a few long backwards strides towards the exit and waved to Ashton, Regina, and Dean.

Before Ashton could respond to Chloe, she had already disappeared out the front door. Ashton inwardly face-palmed herself. *Smooth, Ashton. Real smooth.*

"Alright!" Noah's voice resounded in the near distance as he came bounding down the staircase. Ashton, Dean, and Regina all stared at him. When Noah hopped off the last step, he grinned at his audience and held out his arms. "How do I look?"

"Like a dweeb," Ashton said. "A tie? Really?"

"I think you look sharp." Dean gave Noah a thumbs up.

"Yes." Regina nodded. "You look very handsome."

Noah's mouth shaped into a widespread smile. "Why thank you, Regina...and Dad." He snarled at Ashton. "Majority rules. I look dope."

Ashton chuckled. "Yeah. No one ever said that."

Noah shrugged. "I just did." He grinned. "And for your information, *sis*, the tie is to make me appear more sophisticated than I already am for my night on the town with Lily. I'm taking her to dinner at some swanky restaurant I found out about online and then we're going to a movie."

"Awe. You're such a gentleman." Ashton pretended to gag.

"I think it's sweet," Regina said.

Noah adjusted the knot of his necktie. "Thank you, Regina." He glanced at his watch then he looked at Dean. "I'm gonna go. Thanks again for letting me borrow your car."

"No problem." Dean tossed a set of keys to Noah. "Bring it back in one piece."

Noah caught the keys and pocketed them. "Of course I will."

"Curfew." Dean's voice was stern.

"Wouldn't miss it." Noah shifted his gaze to Ashton. "Later."

Ashton lifted her hand in a faux wave. "Later, bro."

Noah pointed to Dean and Regina using both of his index fingers. "Goodnight!" He turned his back to the three of them and swiftly left the house.

Several seconds of silence hovered over Ashton, Dean, and Regina until Ariel shook her rattle. Regina smiled warmly at the baby then squeezed Dean's arm. "Ready?"

Dean patted his wife's hand. "I'm ready." He eyed Ashton. "Do you need anything before we go?"

"I'm all set," Ashton said.

"Alright. We'll see you in a few hours." He neared his daughter.

Ashton sidestepped her father to avoid the hug he was about to give her. She punched him light-heartedly on his right shoulder. "Yep. See ya."

Dean quickly twisted his frown into a tight smile. "Have a good evening."

"That's the plan."

When Dean and Regina got to the door, Dean looked back at Ashton. "Don't do anything crazy now." He chuckled.

Ashton rolled her eyes. "As if."

***

Ashton glanced down at the baby cradled in her arms when the credits began to roll to the movie she had been watching.

"And that, kiddo, was *The Mermaid that Could*. Supposedly you were named after the main character, Ariel, who is by far the coolest mermaid in the film."

The child stared at Ashton.

"Good talk," Ashton said.

Ariel's small mouth formed a tiny smile.

Ashton laughed. "I can't tell if you're genuinely smiling at me or you just have gas, but I'm choosing to believe that it's a smile." She sighed and touched Ariel's nose with the tip of her finger. "Well, you *are* a cute baby. I'll give you that, but don't tell anyone I said that." Ashton studied the child's features. "You have your sister's eyes. Not me. Your other sister...which is a compliment really because she has very pretty eyes. They're sorta like this brown color, but an intense brown. Almost black." She nodded. "Definitely intense," Ashton mumbled dreamily.

Ariel gurgled, snapping Ashton out of her trance. Ashton cleared her throat. "Right. But I digress. In truth, there's a likelihood that you have a teeny bit of each of us about you. After all, we are family."

The baby gurgled again.

"Yeah. I love you too, kid." Ashton peered around Ariel's dimly lit room. "We should get you to bed though."

"Do you want help with that?" Chloe's voice came from behind.

Ashton's heart slammed to a halt. It took her a moment to find air, but once she did, a shaky exhale escaped her. She rose from the rocking chair and slowly turned around with the baby still in her arms. Chloe was standing in the doorway, hands tucked inside the front pockets of her jeans. She tipped her head to the side and smiled, her brown irises shimmering in the near-darkness. Ashton's body temperature instantly spiked.

"Hi." Chloe spoke softly.

"Yeah. Hi." Ashton looked to Ariel then to Chloe. "You know you really shouldn't sneak up on people when they're holding a baby. I could've dropped her."

Chloe chuckled and crossed her arms over chest. "You wouldn't have dropped her."

"But I could've. You scared me."

Chloe pouted. "I didn't mean to scare you. I'm sorry."

Ashton shrugged. "It's fine."

"So did you want help putting her to bed?"

"Um. I think I can manage. Thanks." Ashton carried Ariel to the crib and gently laid her down. She draped a blanket over the baby and gave the mobile hanging above the child's bed a spin. "Sleep tight, kiddo." Ashton switched the monitor on and put her part of the device in the pocket of her hooded sweatshirt. She cautiously doubled back to where Chloe was.

"You're good with her," Chloe noted. "It's cute."

Ashton ignored the compliment. "Why are you home so early? It's hours until curfew."

"Because this is where I want to be." Without looking away from Ashton, Chloe picked up the remote control from the table next to the rocking chair, aimed it at the television and shut it off. She put the controller down and held out her hand. "Come with me?"

Ashton swallowed hard. "What for? Where are we going?"

"Take my hand and you'll find out."

Ashton's eyes narrowed and she tentatively placed her hand in Chloe's.

Chloe grinned and nodded towards the exit before she started moving toward it, delicately ushering Ashton out of Ariel's room and into the hallway. When they reached the door to Chloe's bedroom, Chloe stopped walking. She turned and leaned against the door, her fingers still wrapped around Ashton's hand.

"So you think my eyes are intense, huh?" The left side of Chloe's closed mouth arced up forming a small smirk.

Ashton bowed her slow-shaking head to hide her scarlet cheeks. "Damnit, Chloe. Do you hear *everything*? How long were standing there?" She timidly looked up at Chloe.

"Long enough." Chloe tightened her grip on Ashton and easily pulled her closer until there were only a few inches separating them.

The next breath Ashton took was shallow and rapid all at once. She could practically taste the sweetness of Chloe's lip balm. After an elongated blink, Ashton met Chloe's unfaltering gaze.

"Are you nervous?" Chloe asked.

"Should I be?"

"No."

"Then no. I'm not."

Chloe smiled a little. "Good." She lifted her free hand and fidgeted with the pendant hanging from Ashton's neck. Ashton's skin prickled. Her palms became dewy.

"You wear it well." Chloe spoke softly.

"Thanks."

"You're welcome." Chloe drew her bottom lip between her teeth. "Can I tell you something?"

"Yes."

"I don't care about safe."

Ashton's throat grew thick. "You don't?"

Chloe's fingers left Ashton's necklace and she traced them along the side of Ashton's face. "No." She ran her thumb over Ashton's slightly parted lips. "So I'm going to invite you into my bedroom now. Okay?"

Ashton's stomach dropped and a raging chill coursed through her. She barely swallowed. "Okay."

With her hand still on Ashton's face, Chloe flattened her palm against Ashton's heated cheek. Chloe's eyelids fluttered as she tipped her head the slightest bit while guiding Ashton's mouth closer to her own. Intuitively, Ashton shut her eyes. As soon as Chloe's lips brushed across Ashton's, Ashton's mouth opened just enough so that the tip of her tongue could caress Chloe's. Chloe's arms immediately wrapped around Ashton's neck as Ashton's hands found their way to the sides of Chloe's face. The kiss quickly deepened in unrestrained eagerness. Ashton pressed herself into Chloe and raked her fingers through Chloe's wavy, honey blonde hair. Breathless, Chloe slowed the kiss and smiled against Ashton's lips. She then reached for the bedroom doorknob with her left hand, gave it a quick jiggle and pushed the door open. She took a step backwards into the room.

"Do you want to come in?" Chloe's voice was husky.

"Yes."

Chloe's brown eyes grew darker. Her pupils dilated. A small grin played on her lips. She grabbed onto the strings attached to Ashton's hoodie and tugged, luring Ashton toward her. Once Ashton passed through the threshold of the room, she blindly felt for the door behind her, got a hold of it and shut it. Coquettishly, she leaned against the white, wooden panel. Then Ashton stretched her arms out a little and grabbed Chloe by her wrists. Chloe inhaled suddenly. She stared at Ashton wantonly and let the strings of Ashton's sweatshirt fall from her grip. Ashton drew Chloe closer. When their knees touched, Ashton released Chloe. Without hesitation, Chloe cupped Ashton's face in her hands and kissed her hard. In seconds, their lips and tongues established a slow, steady, faultless rhythm. But when Chloe's hands began to drift from Ashton's face, down her sides and to the button of Ashton's jeans, their kiss became more frantic. Their breathing erratic. Chloe deftly unfastened Ashton's pants and then she latched onto the hem of Ashton's pullover. Chloe's satiny lips found Ashton's neck. Ashton's throat released a titillating sigh as she tilted her head back against the door. Dizzy with lust, Ashton managed to slip the monitor from the pocket of her sweatshirt and placed it on top of the dresser to her left.

"You good?" Chloe murmured into Ashton's ear before playfully biting her earlobe.

"I'm good," Ashton breathed.

Chloe traced her tongue along Ashton's jawline and kissed the corner of Ashton's mouth. "Arms up," she instructed.

Still pinned against the door, Ashton raised her arms as Chloe expertly removed her hoodie and tossed it aside, leaving Ashton's upper body covered only by a black, muscle tank top and a low-cut, cotton bra of the same color. Chloe paused for a moment and drank in Ashton's figure. The heat in Chloe's eyes nearly melted Ashton. Then Chloe glided her hands slowly across Ashton's clothed breasts, eliciting a soft gasp from Ashton. Chloe bit her bottom lip through a wicked grin and pulled off Ashton's shirt. She backed away a few inches, her animalistic gaze roamed over Ashton and she inhaled sharply. "You're so fucking beautiful," Chloe whispered when her focus fell on Ashton's face. The girls stared intently into one another's eyes for a lasting second during which Chloe's fingertips charted along all of Ashton's scars. Ashton fought not to flinch. "Every single part of you." Chloe stretched each word, smiled kindly at Ashton, and kissed her softly on the lips. Once. Then she coaxed Ashton's mouth open with her tongue and kissed her again. Fervently. Ashton indulged the kiss with matching urgency. Their mouths moved skillfully in time with each other's. In between short, manic intakes of air, Ashton began to work the buttons on Chloe's navy blue short sleeved blouse. When she wrestled the last one undone, Ashton slipped Chloe's shirt off her shoulders, revealing a lacey orchid colored bra. Chloe's hands found Ashton's waist and she pulled Ashton into her. Without interrupting the kiss, Chloe began stepping backwards, clumsily steering herself and Ashton over to the bed. Once Chloe's calves bumped against the mattress, Ashton's lips started traveling along Chloe's neck, her collarbone, her cleavage. She reached behind Chloe and unfastened Chloe's bra. Ashton's fingers lightly grazed Chloe's bare breasts. She teasingly tweaked Chloe's hard nipples between her thumbs and forefingers. Chloe's breath caught audibly.

Ashton's hands landed on the small of Chloe's back. "Lay down," Ashton rasped as she slowly lowered Chloe onto the bed. Chloe roped her arms around Ashton's neck before kissing her hungrily while silently directing Ashton down with her. Ashton followed Chloe's lead, crawling on top of her. Using her right arm, Ashton held herself up, hovering above Chloe. With her left hand, Ashton unsnapped Chloe's jeggings and together, they wriggled the pants off Chloe. Ashton's fingertips then toured the length of Chloe's inner thighs. Ashton slowed the pace of their kiss and brought it to a cessation. She opened her eyes and took in Chloe's silken, alabaster skin until each curve of Chloe's body was etched in her memory. She gazed into the ebony hues of Chloe's eyes. Chloe gently placed her palm on Ashton's cheek and smiled at her. Neither of them spoke, but somehow they both understood. Ashton just smiled back at Chloe and with ease, resumed kissing her. As the dance between their lips and tongues gradually became more frenzied, Chloe nimbly discarded Ashton's bra. Chloe teased Ashton's nipples with her thumbs and the ache between Ashton's legs continued to build. Then Chloe's hands glided down Ashton's sides until they reached Ashton's jeans. With one quick pull, Chloe succeeded in getting Ashton's pants below her hips. With surprising agility, Chloe used her right foot to push Ashton's jeans down to her ankles. She toyed with the rim of Ashton's bikini underwear in an act of flirtatious torment before her determined hands dismissed them entirely. Ashton shivered though a thin layer of sweat coating her body. Greedily, Ashton slipped Chloe's V-string panties off. Now that both girls were completely undressed, their naked bodies began writhing together in perfect synchronicity. In a languid-like motion, Ashton slid her left hand between Chloe's thighs and smoothed her forefinger over Chloe's wet center. Chloe peeled her mouth away from Ashton's for air and a soft moan escaped her. Her heart ruthlessly pounding, Ashton ran her fingers over Chloe's sex again. Then again. Chloe started rocking her hips back and forth in time with Ashton's movements and that's when Ashton slid her fingers inside of Chloe. Chloe gasped and looked up into Ashton's glimmering gray eyes. Ashton imparted a warm but almost wolfish smile to her. Chloe bit her lip, shut her eyes and tilted her head back further into the mattress. Ashton's fingers pulsed steadily inside Chloe as her lips and tongue explored Chloe's body: her breasts, her abdomen, the curves of waist, her pelvis. Ashton carefully eased herself out of Chloe. She sat up on her knees, removed the elastic that she had been wearing on her wrist and quickly tied her long, brown loose curls up into a messy ponytail. Her fingers artfully reentered Chloe as she dipped her down between Chloe's legs. Chloe's fingernails found Ashton's shoulders and she scratched them, her breaths were rapid and low. Ashton kissed Chloe's inner thighs and then brushed her tongue over Chloe's clitoris. She savored the taste of Chloe for a second before she began diligently circling and caressing the source of Chloe's arousal with her tongue. Suddenly, Chloe's breathing near stopped. Her muscles tensed. Her body shook. And a ragged exhale slipped from the depths of her throat. When Chloe's body slackened, Ashton slithered her way upwards until her face aligned with Chloe's. The girls' eyes met and Ashton softly kissed Chloe's lips. Chloe touched Ashton's left cheek, smiling a gentle smile.

"Do you trust me?" Chloe whispered.

"I do."

"Good." Chloe skimmed Ashton's lips with her tongue in a beckoning manner. Ashton's mouth opened slightly in response. For several seconds, their lips and tongues lightly taunted one another's until both girls became restless. Their mouths crashed ravenously into each other's in a passionate kiss that grew more feverish with every passing moment. Using the weight of her body, Chloe carefully rolled Ashton over so that Ashton was now lying on her back. Without interrupting the kiss, Chloe maneuvered herself on top of Ashton. Only then did Chloe unhurriedly pull her mouth away from Ashton's. She began to explore. Chloe's hot breath tickled Ashton's neck. Then Chloe used the tip of her tongue to taste Ashton's sweat-dampened porcelain skin, sending a jolt through Ashton that nearly shook her bones. Then, one by one, Chloe took Ashton's breasts into her mouth. Ashton gasped several times, trying to catch her breath. She entangled her fingers in Chloe's blonde bob as Chloe's tongue traversed along Ashton's torso all the way to the space between her thighs. When Chloe slowly drew her tongue across Ashton's slick center, Ashton let out a low moan and pulled on Chloe's hair a little. Chloe tasted Ashton again, careful to lick around Ashton's clit enough to make Ashton's body tighten and relax in all the right places. Bit by bit, Chloe started to crawl back on top of Ashton. When their bodies aligned, they stared at each other but only briefly before Chloe pressed her mouth hard against Ashton's for a long minute. When she broke away, both girls were left breathless.

"I promise I won't hurt you," Chloe husked.

Ashton bit her bottom lip and nodded.

Chloe grinned and eased herself up into a kneeling position, one of Ashton's legs on either side of her. She kept her eyes fixed on Ashton as she smoothed her palms over Ashton's inner thighs. Unconsciously, Ashton tilted her pelvis upward. Chloe's black irises grew darker. Her grin disappeared. Almost leisurely, she slid her right forefinger along with her middle finger inside Ashton. Ashton's chest locked as Chloe began pulsating Ashton's g-spot. She closed her eyes, clenched her jaw, and swallowed whatever air she could. With her left hand, Chloe used her fingertips to massage Ashton's clitoris while adding a third digit inside Ashton.

"Fuck," Ashton groaned, grabbing at the sheets.

Chloe's movements gained momentum and she applied more pressure. Ashton warmed all over as a pleasurable force ripped through her body. The sound of Chloe's soft but heavy breaths made Ashton wetter. The throbbing within Ashton peaked. A tingling sensation coursed through her and her muscles contracted. Ashton's body seized momentarily and then she tremored as a quiet moan slipped from somewhere deep inside her. While her breathing struggled to normalize, Ashton gripped Chloe's left hand to keep it still. Wearily, Ashton opened her eyes and gazed up at Chloe. She smiled lazily. Chloe smiled back and leaned forward, resting her body flat against Ashton's. Their flesh melded together. Chloe swept her lips across Ashton's.

"Your eyes are all sparkly," Chloe spoke softly.

"Because I'm looking at you."

"Oh. Is that why?"

"That *is* why."

Chloe lightly touched the side of Ashton's face. "Of all the girls, you sparkle for me, huh?"

"Mmhmm."

"I love it." Chloe pursed her lips and nodded. "Yup. I'm definitely digging that."

Ashton chuckled. "So I guess we're more than friends now."

"Don't be silly." Chloe kissed Ashton's cheek. "We've always been more than friends."

"I know."

***

After lying on Chloe's bed, wrapped in each other's arms for what could have been an hour...or several, Chloe stirred, lifted her head from Ashton's shoulder, and broke the serene silence surrounding them.

"Hey Ashton," Chloe husked.

Ashton opened her eyes and smiled. "Hi."

Chloe returned the smile. "Hi." She rested her left hand on Ashton's bare chest. "We should get up."

Ashton frowned.

Chloe laughed a little. "I feel that way too, but Dean and my Mom will probably be home soon. It might be in our best interest if we're not just chillin' in the buff when they arrive."

Ashton sighed exasperatingly. "Ugh. But I like it here."

Chloe ran her fingertips over Ashton's skin. "I like you here." She chewed on her bottom lip. "You're welcome to come back...you know, if you wanted to. Or not. It's entirely up to you. There's no pressure."

Ashton raised her eyebrows at Chloe. "Chloe. My gosh. Are *you* nervous?"

"Pssht." Chloe's protest was short-lived and she pouted. "Okay. Fine. Maybe I'm a smidge nervous."

"Why?"

Chloe lowered her gaze. "Because there's a chance you'll end up regretting this."

"That's not going to happen."

"You can't be sure of that."

"Yes. I can be and I am." Ashton reached up and touched Chloe's face. "If anyone has a reason to be worried here, it's *me*."

Chloe rolled her eyes. "Why do you say that?"

"For reasons such as Erin and Trevor."

Chloe nodded slowly. "Yeah. About that." She inhaled deeply. "Before I came home earlier tonight, I ended things with both of them."

Ashton's mouth fell open and she quickly closed it. "You did?"

"Yup."

"Why did you...why?"

Chloe stared into Ashton's eyes. "I had to. My feelings for you were too strong. I had no idea if anything romantic was actually going to happen between us or not, but every time I was with either of them I felt like I was cheating on you." She shrugged. "Like something in me is loyal to you. Only you. It's the weirdest thing."

Ashton swallowed. "Good weird or bad weird?"

Chloe smirked. "Fantastic weird. Obvi."

Ashton released a relieved chuckle. "What does all that mean to you?"

"It depends."

"On what?"

"On your answer."

Ashton's forehead creased. "What's the question?"

"Ashton, will you..." Chloe took a deep breath. "Will you be with me?"

"I am with you. I'm right here. See?" Ashton outstretched her arms.

The corners of Chloe's mouth turned down. "Don't joke. I'm being serious."

Ashton held onto Chloe's hips. "Alright. I'm sorry." She kissed Chloe's chin. "Ask me again."

"Will you be with me?"

"In what way?"

Chloe gaped. "Ashton! Really?"

"Yes really. Casually or—"

Chloe pressed her lips against Ashton's to keep Ashton from finishing her thought. Once Chloe pulled away, she shook her head. "No. Not casually."

"Then how?"

"In all the ways." Chloe bestowed Ashton with a lopsided smile. "Will you be with me in all the ways?"

"Monogamously?"

"That's right."

"This is what you truly want?" Ashton asked.

"Mmhmm. It is my truest want." Chloe grinned.

Ashton cupped Chloe's face in her hands and beamed. "Yes. Of course I will be with you."

"In all the ways?"

"In all the ways."

Chapter Twenty-One

"I can't believe you missed our Instavisit date last night!" Katlyn pouted into her laptop's camera at Ashton.

"I'm sorry."

"You better have an amazing excuse like you had super hot sex or something."

Ashton's cheeks heated. She winced and bowed her head slightly, fighting off a guilty smile. "Well..."

"Oh my lord! You *did* have sex last night! You little harlot, you!"

Ashton chuckled and shook, her head back and forth as she stared at her computer screen. "No. It's not like that. And I am NOT a harlot."

"Settle down, my friend. You know I'm just fucking with you." Katlyn's eyes suddenly widened. "Holy mother! Was it with Chloe? Please tell me it was with Chloe."

"A lady never tells."

"Ha! That's a dead giveaway! Gimme all the deets."

"Kat, no."

"Why not?"

"Because a lady never tells."

"Aargh! That's bullshit! A lady always tells especially if she's talking to her bestie, so start talking, missy."

Ashton sighed. "We're dating now...Chloe and me."

Katlyn grinned. "Well it's about goddamned time! Alright so when did this all happen? When did you two become a thing?"

"Umm. Last night."

"Before or after you slept together?"

"Dude, the timeline doesn't matter so please drop it, okay?"

"Ugh. Fiiine," Katlyn droned.

"Thank you."

"You're welcome." Katlyn cleared her throat. "Chloe and Ashton sitting in a tree k-i-s-s-i-n-g," she sang.

"Wow. Your maturity level is through the roof," Ashton deadpanned.

"I'm just really excited for you! You have a girlfriend! You're actually dating the girl you've been fawning over."

"I wasn't fawning."

"Pssht. You were fawning." Kat tipped her head to the side. "Do Regina or Dean know?"

"No! Are you nuts?!"

"Well you said it went down last night. Is there a chance they could have seen you two together when they got home?"

"Nope. We were very careful," Ashton said. "After we...uh...so before they came home, I went back into my bedroom, which is where they found me when they got in. Chloe was downstairs watching television...or pretending to. They suspected nothing."

Katlyn pursed her lips. "Huh. Are you gonna tell them?"

Ashton shrugged. "Eventually I guess we have to, but Chloe and I didn't discuss it yet."

"But you're both on the same page about it? That Regina and Dean should know?"

"Yeah. We are."

"Alright." Katlyn nodded. "Did you tell Noah?"

"Not yet. I haven't figured out how to tell him."

"Um. Saying the words is usually a good way to go."

Ashton rolled her eyes. "If only it were that simple." She took a deep breath. "Even though he supports me...and my feelings for Chloe...it's still weird for him. He was never shy about his thoughts on the whole thing. He's been trying to be more open-minded for my sake, but..." Ashton paused and worried her bottom lip. "So it's going to be...awkward maybe? Definitely hard. Ugh. Just thinking about it stresses me out."

"Maybe you're better off if you tell him sooner rather than later that way you're not carrying it around on the brink of an anxiety attack. Just sayin'."

"I'll feel it out."

"So in the meantime, this is one big secret?"

Ashton nodded, frowning. "Yeah. Until Chloe and I decide it's time to come out."

"You guys are just gonna be sneaking around, having this like secret love affair?"

"For now."

Katlyn shrugged. "Okay. It's your life. I'll back you with whatever you do."

"Thanks, Kat."

"Sure." Katlyn narrowed her eyes. "What about the other people Chloe was seeing?"

A small smile tugged at the corners of Ashton's mouth. "She ended things with them."

"Monogamy? Wow. She must really dig you, you sexy thang."

Both girls shared a light-hearted laugh.

"I dig her too," Ashton said.

"I'm aware."

"Oh! And I asked her to the concert...she said yes." Ashton grinned.

"Woot!"

"I'm excited."

Katlyn smiled. "Good." Her pleased disposition quickly faded. "Hey, Ash...uh...what are you two going to do when the summer's over and you come back here to Florida?"

Ashton's expression saddened. "We haven't gotten that far yet. I'm unsure of how to broach that topic."

"Because you're scared?"

"Of course I'm scared, Katyln." Ashton pressed her right hand against her forehead for a moment then stared at her friend. "We *just* got together. I don't want to lose her."

"Then don't. Don't lose her. And get on that broaching shit. You hear?"

"I hear you. I'll talk to her the next time I see her."

"When's that?"

"No clue. Dude, it's only eight o'clock in the morning." Ashton glanced down at the bottom of her computer screen. "Fuck."

"What?"

"Everyone is going to start gathering in the kitchen soon for breakfast."

"And that's bad why?"

"If she's there and they're all there I...I don't know how to do this. I need a plan," Ashton said.

"No, buddy. What you need is to come out."

Ashton groaned. "I know. I know you're right."

"Well, duh. I'm a genius. What do you expect?"

Ashton glared at Katlyn. "Why does this have to be so hard?"

"Because life is hard...I mean if you're truly living it, which you want to do, don't you?"

"Yes."

"Then stop stalling cuz you're afraid and go do what you gotta do to get through this. Go live."

Before Ashton could respond, Katlyn waved and quickly said, "luv ya!" Then the screen went black.

***

Ashton closed her laptop and got off her bed, where she had been sitting while chatting with Katlyn online. She smoothed her hands over her t-shirt as she neared the full-length mirror on the bathroom door. Ashton faced her reflection and pouted. She combed her fingers through her long, tousled hair, which was still damp from the shower she had taken earlier this morning. She touched the pendant hanging from her neck that Chloe had given her, and took a deep breath. She then stepped out of the bathroom and strolled towards the exit of her room. "Everything will be okay," Ashton told herself while making her exit.

As soon as Ashton entered the hall, she peered over at Chloe's bedroom door. Before she could look away, Chloe emerged from her room and their eyes immediately locked. Chloe smiled.

"Good morning."

Ashton couldn't help but smile back. "Good morning."

Chloe glanced around the area. The hallway was empty. Her gaze returned to Ashton and she padded slowly to where Ashton was standing. She stopped when there were still several feet between them. "I thought about you all night," she whispered.

Ashton stared down at her sneakers as a deep blush spread across her cheeks. She nodded. "I thought about you too." Her eyes found Chloe again. "We have to talk though."

Chloe paled. "About what? What's wrong?"

With cautious agility, Ashton reached out her hand and brushed it against Chloe's. "Nothing's wrong. I swear."

"Okay. What then?"

"They need to know." Ashton tipped her head in the direction of the staircase. Several voices could be heard from the dining room. "Dean, Regina, Noah..."

Chloe sucked in a breath. "Right."

"What should we do?"

Chloe pressed her lips tightly together. "Um. Alright. How about for now, we act like we usually act. Try to be inconspicuous and stuff until we figure out what to do."

"Okay."

"Okay." Chloe motioned to the stairs. "Do you want to go down first or do you want me to? We never go down for breakfast together."

Ashton frowned. "I already hate this."

"Me too, but it's just for now."

"I know." Ashton lost herself in Chloe's dark gaze for a moment. "I want to kiss you," she spoke softly.

Chloe grinned, quickly scanned the halls once more then grabbed Ashton by the collar of her t-shirt and pulled her in for a kiss that left them both panting. Chloe bit her bottom lip and shook her head, smirking. "Please tell me we can do more of that later."

"We can absolutely do more of that later."

"Good." Chloe ran her thumb over Ashton's mouth. "I got lipstick on you. Sorry."

"No you're not."

"No. I'm not." Chloe winked. "Okay. I'll go down there first. Give me about three minutes and then come down. We'll play it like we haven't seen each other yet this morning. If anything comes up, which I doubt it will since they spoke to each of separately last night, I'll handle it and you follow my lead. Alright?"

"Got it."

"And I'll text you after breakfast about meeting up."

"Okay."

Chloe smiled sideways and began making her way to the stairs. She placed her right foot on the top step then turned to Ashton. "Hey."

"Yeah?"

"While we're eating breakfast, you might like to know that I'm really wet for you right now." Chloe's eyes flashed mischievously.

Ashton's face heated as her stomach flip-flopped. "Thanks."

"My pleasure," Chloe said. "See you in a few." She blew Ashton a kiss and descended to the first floor.

When Chloe was out of sight, Ashton inhaled Chloe's lingering scent and sighed. "Nope. Definitely my pleasure," she uttered.

Chapter Twenty-Two

After a breakfast filled with secret smiles and low-profile gazes between Ashton and Chloe, Ashton headed back up to her room to await Chloe's text message about when they could hang out next. Just as Ashton went to reach for the doorknob, Noah grabbed her arm.

"Hold up there," Noah spoke softly. "What was that about?"

Ashton pushed Noah's grip away. "What was what about?"

"You and Chloe at breakfast." Noah widened his eyes for emphasis. "I saw all the little cutesy looks you kept giving each other. And don't think for a second that I didn't feel you kick her foot under that table." He put his index finger in his mouth and made a gagging sound.

Ashton gaped. "I did no such thing."

"Dude! I sit *right* beside you and she sits across from you. It was kinda obvious what was going on." Noah's stare grew serious. "So?"

Ashton sighed heavily. "Promise not to say anything?"

"Yes. I promise."

"We're sort of dating. Officially." A slow grin played on Ashton's mouth.

Noah wagged his finger at his sister. "Ah ha! I knew it!" He chuckled and gave Ashton a light punch in her shoulder. "That's my sister...the lady catcher."

"Pfft." Ashton rolled her eyes. "I'm begging you to never call me that again. In fact, don't ever even use the phrase again. Ever."

"Whatevs." Noah crossed his arms over his chest and leaned against the hallway wall next to Ashton's bedroom door. "Are you going to tell Mom and Dad and Regina?"

"Wait. You're not bothered by this? Like at all?"

"No. Ash, I was the one who told you to go for this."

"I know but saying something and then having something be real are two different things and I wasn't sure if, now that it's real, you'd get weirded out."

Noah shrugged. "Well I'm not bothered or weirded out or anything. I'm happy for you."

"You are?"

"Of course I am."

"Thanks, bro."

"Don't mention it." Noah raised an eyebrow. "So...are you gonna come clean to everyone?"

"Someday, yes."

"Someday? Really? What is that supposed to mean? Today? Tomorrow? In another lifetime?"

"I wish it were in another lifetime." Ashton shook her head slightly. "But I know it needs to be soon."

"Worried?"

"Uhh. Yeah!"

"It'll be fine."

"You don't know that," Ashton said.

"No. I don't, but my gut tells me it'll be okay."

"And what if you're gut is wrong and it's not okay?" Ashton fired back.

"I'll stand by you two."

"You will?"

"Yes. You're my sister and even though you piss me off all the time, I love you."

Ashton threw herself into her brother's arms and hugged him tightly. "I love you, too, dipshit."

***

For the third time, Ashton read the text she received from Chloe less than a minute ago.

Keep your door unlocked. I'll be there in about five minutes. You should be naked. Just a suggestion. XO.

Ashton smiled to herself and held the phone on top of her chest. She hadn't locked the door since returning to her bedroom after breakfast in the event that

Chloe stopped by for one of her infamous unannounced visits. She rose to a seated position on her bed, closed her eyes and unconsciously placed her two middle fingers on her lips, recollecting the softness of Chloe's mouth pressed against her own. Ashton's heart roared excitedly. When a knock at her door pulled Ashton from her daydream, her heart temporarily stopped beating altogether.

"It's open," Ashton called out.

The doorknob turned slowly and Mr. Daniels stood in the entrance of Ashton's room. Ashton's mouth went dry.

"Ashton, hi. How are you?" Mr. Daniels asked.

"Um. Good." Ashton nodded. "I'm good. Yourself?"

Dean smiled. "I'm well." He stepped further into the room. Ashton internally grimaced. "I wanted to thank you again for babysitting last night."

"Pfft. That?" Ashton waved away her father's words as she got to her feet. "Don't mention it."

"It meant a lot. It deserves mentioning." Dean glanced around Ashton's room. "I was on my way to the farmer's market for some fresh produce. I wanted to ask you if you were interested in joining me."

Without warning, Chloe appeared in the hallway right outside of Ashton's bedroom, behind Mr. Daniels. Ashton's eyes widened.

"Ashton?" Dean said.

Ashton swallowed and faced her father. "Huh?"

"Are you sure you're alright?"

"Positive."

"Okay. Then did you want to come with me?" Dean asked.

"Oh. That. Right." Ashton winced. "I can't. I sort of have plans."

"Really?" Mr. Daniels grinned. "That's great! Did you meet someone?"

A drop of sweat trickled down Ashton's spine. "Uhhh." She glanced at Chloe in a panic.

"Hey, Dean," Chloe's voice interjected as she moved closer to the entryway of Ashton's room. She lingered in the doorway.

Dean swiveled around and laughed a short, slightly startled laugh. "Chloe. Hi. I didn't see you there."

"Sorry. I didn't mean to frighten you," Chloe said.

"No. It's fine. You didn't frighten me."

Chloe's eyes fell on Ashton. She raised her arm and tapped her wrist as if she were wearing a watch. "Ready? We don't want to be late."

Dean then looked quizzically at Ashton. "Chloe is...you two have plans together?"

"Yeah." Ashton gave Chloe a quick smile. "I'm ready."

Dean shook his head, confused, before he scrutinized Chloe and then Ashton. "You girls are friends?"

"That's one way to put it." Chloe flashed Ashton a smirk. Ashton glared at Chloe and cleared her throat.

Mr. Daniels pursed his lips. "Oh."

"What?" Ashton inquired.

"Nothing. I just got the impression that you two didn't...never mind." Dean forced a smile to mask his bewilderment. "I'm glad you're friendly with each other."

"Sooo it's cool?" Ashton asked Dean. "That we're hanging out and stuff?"

Mr. Daniels nodded. "Absolutely. It's very cool." He moved closer to the exit of the room. "Well, I'll leave you girls to it. Have fun. Call or text if you won't be home for dinner."

"We will," Chloe assured.

Mr. Daniels was still nodding. "Okay. Good. This is good." He spoke under his breath and vanished from Ashton's room.

Ashton frowned and looked to Chloe. "That was crazy awkward. We should have told him then."

"I agree. That was a billion percent awkward and we'll tell him. Now wasn't the time though," Chloe said.

"When is the time then?"

Chloe held out her hand to Ashton. "We're going to figure that out together. Does that work for you?"

Ashton slipped her hand into Chloe's. "Together," she repeated softly. "That definitely works for me."

***

"I just think the sooner we do it, the less painful it will be," Ashton said quietly.

Chloe reached across the small table the two girls were seated at inside The Bean and took Ashton's hand. "What makes you think it's going to be painful?"

"Why wouldn't it be? It's a very...odd situation. I mean, to Dean and your mom, we're like sisters in some blended family sort of way. What if Dean's mind isn't as open as I thought? Like he was cool about my being gay and such, but this is...it could be too much; asking him to accept that his daughter and his step-daughter are involved."

Chloe gaped. "We're involved?"

Ashton stared piercingly at Chloe. "Really? You're making jokes."

"Yes because you're only focusing on the worst case scenario and it's stressing you out. Neither of us knows what's going to happen, but it might not be as bad as you're anticipating," Chloe said. "Besides I'm quite besotted with you and maybe I enjoyed repeating the fact that we're actually 'involved.'" She batted her lashes.

Ashton's cheeks warmed and she furnished a small smile.

Chloe gave Ashton's hand a squeeze then ran her thumb over Ashton's knuckles. "It's adorbs how you blush so easily. It makes me want to kiss you."

Ashton's jaw became taut. She swallowed back her nerves and looked into Chloe's dark, hypnotic eyes. "Then kiss me."

Chloe narrowed her gaze. "Seriously?"

"Mmhmm."

Chloe moved her other arm onto the table and on bent elbows, she inched her upper body closer to Ashton. When Chloe was close enough for Ashton to smell the coffee on her breath, Ashton shut her eyes. Chloe's full, velvety lips swept across Ashton's slowly and as quickly as their mouths met, the kiss was over, leaving Ashton deprived of oxygen and yearning for more. Chloe sat back down in her chair and grinned at Ashton before taking a sip of her beverage.

Ashton pouted. "Tease."

"Well yeah. To keep you interested."

"Chloe, I'm always interested when it comes to you."

Chloe shrugged. "You could lose interest. You never know."

"I won't. I know."

"There's no way for you to know."

Ashton lifted Chloe's hand to her mouth and kissed it. "Then there's no way for you to know I'm wrong."

Chloe chuckled lightly and nodded. "Clever."

"Eh. Not really, buuut if you decide you want to follow through with that kiss later on, I'm so down for that."

"Noted."

Ashton sighed. "But until then, we need to figure out what to do with Dean and Regina."

"Agreed." Chloe took another sip of her coffee. "At least Noah's behind us."

"Yeah. He's a good guy when he wants to be." Ashton shifted in her seat. "I'm sorry I told him without telling you that I was going to tell him. He did this sneak attack thing and cornered me. I panicked and outed us."

Chloe smiled. "It's okay. I'm glad he knows."

"Me too."

"Alright so you want to get this over with on the sooner side." Chloe took a deep breath. "How about we tell them today when we get back to the house?"

An influx of nausea assailed Ashton's stomach. "Today?"

"Yeah. Today."

"That's super soon."

Chloe arched an eyebrow at Ashton. "You said you wanted it to be done soon. Today is soon but then it will be over with."

"Okay. You're right. You're right. We can do this."

"We can. And regardless of how they react, I still want to be...involved with you." Chloe smirked. "If you want that too."

"Of course I want that."

"No matter what?"

"No matter what."

Chapter Twenty-Three

"So you wanted to talk to us?" Dean crossed his left leg over his right and leaned back into the plush sofa cushion, looking attentively at Chloe, who was standing a few feet away from him in the center of the living room.

Chloe nodded in response to the question and then faced her mother, sitting next to Dean. "Mom, you always said that it's important that you and Dean meet anyone that I'm...um...involved with, which is why I wanted us all to sit down together." She swallowed. "I have something to tell you."

Dean glimpsed behind Chloe at the loveseat, where Noah and Ashton were seated beside one another. "Well this must be a very important person if you wanted the whole family to know about them." His eyes returned to Chloe.

Ashton shrunk into herself and folded her hands on her lap. Noah knocked his knee against Ashton's and when she glanced at him, he gave her a small, supportive smile. Ashton couldn't smile back. She brought her sights back to Chloe, Dean, and Regina and waited because that's all she could do. Wait. This is how she and Chloe agreed to come out as a couple. Every single muscle in Ashton's body wanted to jump up, grab Chloe, and run. Instead, she sat there quietly. Waiting.

"Yes," Chloe continued as she wrung her hands together. "This person is very special."

Suddenly, Regina's face lit up. "Are you engaged?!"

Chloe let out a nervous laugh and shook her head. "No, Mom. It's not that."

"Honey, just let her speak," Dean said to Regina.

Regina's smile waned. "Sure. I'm sorry, sweetheart," she said to Chloe. "Go on with what you were saying."

"Right. Okay." Chloe cleared her throat. "I'm no longer seeing Erin or Trevor because I'm exclusively dating someone." She took a couple of steps backwards towards the loveseat.

Riddled with doubt, Ashton shakily rose to her feet. Chloe took Ashton's hand.

"I'm exclusively dating Ashton," Chloe declared.

The living room became silent. Regina and Dean stared blankly at Chloe and Ashton. After what seemed like years, Regina opened her mouth, her brow furrowed and she shook her head adamantly. "No," she said.

"Mom, it's alright," Chloe assured.

Regina sprung from the sofa and pointed her finger at her daughter. "No! This is not alright! I do not approve of this."

Ashton shot her father a pleading look. Dean stood up and placed his hand on Regina's shoulder. "Regina, let's all talk about this calmly."

Regina smacked Dean's hand away and glared at him. "How do you expect me to be calm?! How in heaven's name are you calm?! Did you not hear what Chloe just said?"

"Yes," Dean replied. "I heard her. But getting upset isn't going to help matters."

"Don't you dare even attempt to tell me how to react to this...this...disgraceful behavior!" Regina yelled.

"I'm not trying to tell you how to react," Dean said.

Regina ignored Dean's words and turned her cold stare back to Chloe and Ashton.

"How is this disgraceful?" Chloe asked her mother.

A short, contemptuous laugh escaped Regina. "You are standing here telling me that you are dating the daughter of the man I married. Ashton is essentially your family and you are in a relationship with her and you are asking me how this is disgraceful? As if it's not obvious? Chloe, what you're doing can almost be classified as incest!"

Chloe gasped. "That is SO not true! Ashton and I are not blood related. What we're doing is in no way incestuous."

Regina's eyes widened in anger. "Incestuous or not, it's sick, Chloe! It's sick and twisted and it's unacceptable!"

Chloe flinched and Ashton held her hand tighter.

Dean waved his arms in the air. "Stop! Everybody stop!" He looked at Ashton and Chloe. "How long has this been going on for?" He asked the girls.

"Not long," Ashton finally spoke. "We thought it would be best to tell you right away rather than having you find out on your own or something."

Mr. Daniels rubbed his forehead with his index finger and thumb. "Jesus," he mumbled.

Noah got up and walked over to Ashton and Chloe. "I don't see the problem," he said. "They're not biologically related and they're both legal, consenting adults." He shrugged. "If they want to be together because it's what makes them happy then why is it even an issue?"

Ashton glimpsed at Noah and mouthed him a "Thank you." He nodded.

"I'm sorry, Noah, but you're not a part of this," Regina said.

"Why is that, *Mother*?" Chloe sneered. "Because he made a logical point?"

"We're all a part of this," Dean corrected Regina. "Son, I appreciate your input but this is something that Regina and I have to sort out with your sister and Chloe."

"There's nothing to sort out!" Regina screeched, nearly hysterical. "Dean, your daughter and my daughter cannot be in a relationship. It's simply wrong!"

"Honey, Noah's right. They're not blood relatives. They're not breaking any laws."

Regina gaped at Dean. "I can't believe you." She scowled at Chloe. "And you. I'm beyond disappointed in you." Her eyes bounced between Ashton and Chloe. "I expect you two to put an end to this now."

"No," Chloe said flatly.

"Excuse me?" Regina put her hands on her hips. "Don't you dare speak to me that way and furthermore, you will not defy me. I am your mother and you live under my roof and so long as you do then you obey my rules."

Chloe folded her arms across her chest. "Technically, it's Dean's roof. After all, he is the one who pays the mortgage sooo..."

"Don't push me, Chloe," Regina warned. "I won't allow this scandal to take place under my roof."

"Fine. Then I'll leave," Chloe said.

"What?" Ashton breathed.

"Oh really? And where will go?" Regina inquired.

"Why do you care?" Chloe fired back at her mother. "If you genuinely cared about me you'd just want me to be happy, but you don't because you worry too much about what other people think."

"You know that I care! I have always supported your unorthodox lifestyle," Regina argued. "But this particular situation is not something I can condone."

Chloe let go of Ashton and balled her hands into fists. "Aargh! Why are you being such a bitch about this?"

Before anyone could say anything else, the sharp sound of Regina's hand colliding against Chloe's face echoed throughout the room. There was a full second of stillness before Dean reached for Regina, who had already pulled her arm back and covered her mouth with her palm. "Chloe." Regina's voice cracked.

Chloe gently touched her red cheek and a low sob left her throat. Ashton went to wrap her arms around Chloe, but Chloe help up her hand to keep a distance between them. "It's okay. I'm going."

"Then I'm coming," Ashton said.

"No." Chloe's teary eyes met Ashton's. "I promised you I wouldn't hurt you and look what I've done? I made this mess. This was my plan and I fucked everything up. I failed you. I'm sorry." Chloe stepped away from Ashton and closer to the exit. "I'm real sorry."

"No! Chloe, wait!" Ashton called as Chloe ran out the door. Instinctively, Ashton started after Chloe, but Noah grabbed her.

"Don't," Noah whispered. "Let her go."

Regina sat down slowly and began to cry. Dean cradled his wife.

Ashton collapsed into her brother's hug. "It can't be over. It's barely even begun."

"It's not over. She needs space. Give her space."

"Then I can go get her?" Ashton asked through a whimper.

"Yes. Then you can go get her. Exactly."

Chapter Twenty-Four

On the long stretch of highway at night, Ashton almost missed the turn, which was hidden amidst an abundance of tall trees; their branches slightly swaying from the easy summer breeze. She guided the steering wheel and soon, the crunching of gravel beneath the tires of her father's sedan was all that could be heard. Ashton spotted the familiar SUV right away and pulled up next to it. She cut the engine, unbuckled her safety belt and eased herself out the vehicle.

Munro Reservation was even more peaceful than Ashton remembered. She inhaled the air and started towards the figure perched on the stone bench by the water. When Ashton reached where Chloe was sitting, she stood quietly behind her.

"How did you know I'd be here?" Chloe's voice was low and weak. She sniffled then wiped her nose with the back of her right hand.

"You said it's where you come to escape." Ashton sat beside Chloe on the bench but kept several inches between them. "After what happened, it makes sense that you'd want to escape." She leaned forward, her arms resting on her legs. The water moved lightly when it was brushed by the wind. "How did you know it was me standing behind you just now? It could've been a serial killer. You should really turn around when you hear someone approaching. I'd be super bummed if someone stole you."

Chloe smiled sadly and looked at Ashton out of the corner of her eye. "Thanks for the safety tip. I knew it was you because I knew. I can feel your presence."

"Is it alright that I came or am I encroaching?"

"Depends. Why did you come?"

Ashton sat up straighter and glanced at Chloe. "Because we agreed that whatever happened, we'd be in it together and then you went off by yourself, which was totally uncool of you, but given the circumstances I won't hold it against you for dipping out, however, that gave me little choice but to hunt you down. You see what I'm saying? I mean, we had a pact. I'm not the pact-breaking kinda girl." Ashton pursed her lips, nodding at her own words. "Is that answer okay with you?"

Chloe finally turned her head to fully face Ashton. "It was a good answer."

"Thank you. So I'm not encroaching then?"

"No. You're not encroaching." Chloe took a deep breath. "I'm sorry I bailed on you. Apparently, I *am* a pact-breaking kinda girl."

"You don't have to apologize. Sometimes circumstances change things and it all happens so fast that we're not even realizing what's happening when it's happening. You know? Neither of us thought it would play out anything like it did. But it did. And in that blink of time, you did what you felt you had to and you left."

"Please don't make excuses for me," Chloe said. "I never should have left without you, but I..." She lowered her head. "I was ashamed that I got you hurt. I put you in harm's way. I did the thing I promised you I wouldn't do and because of that, because of me, there's more pain in your life."

"Chloe, no. You didn't add any pain to my life."

"Yes. I did." Chloe glimpsed up at the sky and a few tears streaked her cheeks. "That was *my* idea to tell them that way and it ended up being a complete disaster. I'm sorry."

Ashton scooched even closer to Chloe on the bench and placed her hand on Chloe's leg. "You don't have to be sorry."

"I do though." Chloe bit her quivering bottom lip for a moment, swallowed and then spoke again. "And my mom...she's never done that before. She's been angry, but she's never..." Chloe gently glided her fingers over the side of her face that got struck earlier. She broke into a soft cry.

Something inside of Ashton's heart cracked and her eyes welled up. She wrapped both of her arms around Chloe. Chloe buried her head against Ashton's chest. Her cry became more of a wounded sobbing. Ashton stroked Chloe's silky hair with one of her hands as she held Chloe tightly with the other. "I won't ask because I know you're not alright, but tell me what I can do to make it better. Please."

"This." Chloe's arms tightened around Ashton's waist. "Just do this."

"Done."

"Ashton?"

"Yeah?"

Chloe peered up at Ashton. "Are you mad at me for leaving?"

"No. I'm not mad."

"It's okay if you are. I deserve it."

"Shh. Chloe, I'm not mad." Ashton kissed the top of Chloe's head.

"I'm afraid to go home."

"You don't have to be afraid. I'll be right there with you," Ashton whispered. "And there's nothing to be afraid of. Dean's processing but he's trying to accept it but he's also consoling your mom. She's really upset with herself for what she did to you. Noah's trying to help them make sense of everything."

"This sucks."

Ashton chuckled lightly. "Yup. It sucks pretty hard, but it won't always suck."

"How do you know?"

"I just know."

"How?"

"I'm a romantic. I have to believe it'll be okay. I have to trust in that."

"Do you still trust me?" Chloe asked timorously.

"Absolutely." Ashton nodded. "With everything I've got."

***

Ashton and Chloe entered the house quietly, their fingers intertwined. Upon closing the door as softly as possible, they came to a standstill. Mr. Daniels was sitting on the bottom step of the large staircase, blocking the girls from heading to either of their bedrooms. His features were haggard. He wiped his hand over his mouth, exhaled and stood up.

"I'm glad you're both safe," Mr. Daniels said.

Chloe scanned the vicinity. "Where's Mom?"

"She's upstairs with the baby. We three need to talk." Dean spoke in a low voice.

Ashton's heart sunk. "What's going on?"

Dean gripped Ashton's left shoulder. "Ashton, you're my daughter and I love you, but..." There was a pregnant pause.

"But what?" Ashton probed.

Dean shook his head. "Regina and I had a long conversation." He glanced at Chloe and then his eyes were on Ashton again. "We're not angry at either of you, but we both agreed that you and Chloe shouldn't be under the same roof. As much as we're trying to accept this...this thing between the two of you girls, we can't go along with it or encourage it by allowing the two of you to live in the same house. I'm sorry."

"Meaning?" Chloe asked.

Dean kept his focus on Ashton. "I spoke to your mother. I explained to her everything that's happened."

Ashton jaw slacked. "You called Mom?! You had no right to do that. This is my life. It was supposed to be me who told her. Not you. Me. Don't you get that?"

"I had to call her as soon as I could," Mr. Daniels said.

"Why?" Ashton glared at her father.

"Because I had to coordinate with her and let her know that you were coming home."

"What?" Chloe and Ashton simultaneously gasped.

"I don't want to go," Ashton said. "Don't I have a say in this decision?"

"No," Dean said. "Regina is uncomfortable with all of this to say the least. She's my wife and I have to stand behind her."

"But I'm your child." Ashton's voice cracked. "What about standing behind me? You tell me you want things to be good between us and then you get your chance to back me up and you don't."

Dean frowned. "It's not that simple."

"Please don't make her go," Chloe interjected, pulling Ashton's hand closer to her.

"This is how it has to be," Dean said.

Ashton's eyes filled with tears. "Dad..."

Dean flinched and his face crumpled.

Ashton went on. "Dad, do something. There has to be another solution."

Mr. Daniels cleared his throat. "Maybe there is, but this is what we've decided on." He nodded. "Your flight leaves at 7 o'clock tomorrow morning. I'll drive you to the airport. Your mom will be there when you arrive to drive you home."

Chloe let go of Ashton's hand and stepped towards Dean. "I'm going with her then."

Dean stared at Chloe. "With what money?"

"I'll get a job."

Dean sighed. "Chloe, you're staying here. This is where your mother wants you."

"And what about where *I* want me?"

"Talk to your mother and me again when you have your own money and can support yourself," Dean said.

Ashton bit down on her shaky bottom lip. She took Chloe's hand again and held it hard. "It's okay."

"No!" Chloe bellowed. "It's not okay! You can't give up! This isn't fair!"

"It's not fair," Ashton agreed. "But there isn't anything we can do about it right now." She inhaled through her nose. "We'll find a way." She looked to her father. "Is Noah coming with me?"

Dean crossed his arms over his chest. "I don't know. He's welcome to stay though."

Ashton's jaw tightened as she nodded. "You're really going to let this happen, aren't you?"

"You should pack your things," Dean said.

Some stray tears ran down Ashton's cheeks, over her lips, and dripped from her chin onto the floor. "Don't ever try to be my dad again because you're not. You never were and you never will be. You're the same guy who just keeps abandoning me when I need him." With her words floating in the air, Ashton pushed past Dean and made her way to the staircase. Dejectedly, she climbed the stairs, but not once did she release Chloe from her grip.

Chapter Twenty-Five

"Sweetie, it's a very complicated matter," Mrs. Daniels said. "And while your father and Regina take time to process this, it's truly just best if you come home to Florida."

Ashton groaned into the phone and glanced over at Chloe, who was sitting on the edge of Ashton's bed mindlessly fidgeting with the zipper on the half-packed suitcase next to her. The door to Ashton's bedroom was open per Dean's request. "But Ma, *you* accept the relationship Chloe and I have, don't you?"

"Yes. I do. We had this talk when you came out to me. You know that I believe no one gets to choose who they feel romantically for."

"So you don't think this whole thing is gross or that we're gross?"

"No, honey. It's slightly eccentric, but eccentric is what makes life interesting. Certainly, neither of you are gross."

"Are you disappointed in me?" Ashton asked.

"Ashton, listen carefully to me. I love you. I want you to have experiences. I want you to follow your heart. I don't want your past to hold you back in any way," Mrs. Daniels said. "If nothing else, I'm proud of you. It takes great courage to go after what you want especially if there are risks involved."

Ashton shook her head and sat beside Chloe, who immediately rested her forehead on Ashton's shoulder. Ashton's bottom lip began to tremble and she bit down on it to suppress an oncoming cry. "But that courage got me nowhere. Now I have to leave Boston and Chloe and her mother aren't speaking and everything is messed up."

Chloe's hand found one of Ashton's and she wrapped her fingers around it. "We'll be okay," she whispered.

"Things are not messed up," Mrs. Daniels said. "This is a bump in the road and sometimes that means you have to take a detour. It doesn't mean that you won't end up where you want to be, it only means that you're going to get to your destination via a different route than what you had originally planned."

"Let me guess: detours make life interesting?" Ashton spoke dryly.

"Precisely! Now you're catching on."

"Ugh. Mom, I don't want to leave here."

"I know, but this is your detour. You have to take it."

Ashton nodded sadly. "Right."

"I'll see you in the morning. Call me when you land."

"Okay."

"Have a safe flight."

"Okay."

"I love you, Ashton."

"I love you too, Mom." Ashton hung up the phone and tossed her cell to the side and folded her arms around Chloe.

"I can't believe they're making me go," Ashton said.

Chloe dried her damp cheeks with her left palm and sat up. She faced Ashton. "I didn't intend for any of this to happen."

"Me either." Ashton raked her fingers through Chloe's hair and tucked the longer pieces of Chloe's bangs behind her ear. "None of this is your fault. We didn't do anything wrong."

"Ashton, I don't want this to be the end for us. I don't want to give up."

Ashton leaned closer, sealing the space between Chloe and herself. Her lips softly grazed Chloe's and she smiled a little. "Good because I'm not giving up on us either."

Chloe returned the smile, filled with as much despair as Ashton's, but also just as hopeful. "So many people crush long distance relationships. We could totes be that couple."

"Yeah, we could be."

"We'll text throughout the day, every day, and Instavisit whenever we can."

"Exactly."

"And I'll start applying for a job to save up that way I'll have enough money to buy a ticket to come see you once you're on winter break. We got this. It's going to work."

"It is," Ashton agreed. "It's going to work."

"It has to work, right?" Chloe's eyes were suddenly full of worry.

"I think if we want it to work bad enough then yes, it has to work."

"Well, I for sure know that I want it." Chloe held Ashton's face in her hands. "I want this, and you, so fucking bad. It's ridiculous. I'm completely smitten with you."

"Then you have me." Ashton kissed Chloe again. "You so fucking have me."

***

Noah pulled into the closest empty parking space he could find nearest the airport entrance. He put the SUV in park. He turned to Ashton, who sat silently in the passenger's seat clutching a used tissue. She stared out the window then at her brother. "Thanks for being the one to drive me."

"You're welcome." Noah tapped the steering wheel. "My offer stands, Ash. I'll go with you."

Ashton dabbed the corners of her eyes with the tissue. "No. You live out the summer here like you wanted. And now you have Lily. You can't just up and go. She'd be crushed."

"I told you I had your back. I meant that."

"I know."

"Then let me go home with you," Noah said. "Lily and I will keep in touch. It'll be fine. She'll understand."

"No." Ashton swallowed and unfastened her seatbelt. "You stay here. Check out some of the colleges you wanted to, spend time with your girlfriend...you know, do fun stuff."

"What will you do?"

Ashton shrugged. "Don't know, but I'll manage."

"Please text me at least every other day."

"I think I can handle that," Ashton said.

"Promise?"

"I promise, but you have to make me a promise too."

"Anything. Name it."

"Promise me that you'll look after Ariel and Chloe. I don't want Ariel ever thinking I deserted her and Chloe might be in rough shape. Please reassure her of how much I'm into her."

Noah smiled. "I think I can handle that."

"Um. And there's one more thing."

"What?"

Ashton reached in her bag and pulled out two tickets. She handed them to Noah. "Will you take Chloe to the Eliza Diamonds concert?"

Noah frowned. "Ugh! Duuude! Seriously?"

"You said you'd do anything."

"Yeah. Yeah. I know what I said."

"Then you'll take her?" Ashton asked.

"Sure. I'll take her to the stupid concert."

"Thank you. You're an alright brother."

Noah rolled his eyes. "You're not half bad for a sister either, which is the ONLY reason I'm going to go to this concert."

Ashton hugged Noah. "I love you, dipshit."

"I love you." Noah ruffled Ashton's hair. "Asswipe."

Ashton got out of the vehicle and slung her bag over her shoulders. After gathering her luggage from the backseat, she stuck her head inside the passenger's side window. "But don't forget, I'm the better twin."

Noah chuckled. "And don't you forget, I'm the better looking twin."

Once Ashton and Noah's brief, shared laughter died, Ashton took a deep breath. "I'll talk to you soon."

"Okay. If you need anything..."

"I know." Ashton knocked on the roof of the vehicle as if finalizing their separation then she gave Noah a half-wave and began walking towards to sliding glass doors of the airport.

Chapter Twenty-Six

"Ugh! I can't believe it's already August," Katlyn groaned as she leaned back on Ashton's bed.

Ashton glimpsed at her phone, sighed and then looked at Katlyn. "Yeah. This summer's gone by fast."

Katlyn gestured to Ashton's cell. "She hasn't called yet?"

Ashton frowned. "No! And it's three o' clock. I've heard from her by this time every day since the day I got back here."

"Maybe her phone's dead."

Ashton glared at Katlyn. "Seriously, Kat?"

"Hey. It's my due diligence being your bestie and all to reassure you that everything's fine and that there's a perfectly good explanation as to why you haven't heard from Chloe...and that you will. Soon."

"What if something's wrong?"

"Noah would've reached out to you. She's fine, Ash. Chloe's probably just busy and will be calling or texting any second now." Katlyn pursed her lips before they spread into a mischievous grin. "But since we're on the topic of Chloe, how are things with you two?"

Ashton rolled her eyes but failed at fighting off a smile. "Good."

"Can I ask you a question?"

"You just did." Ashton stuck her tongue out at Katlyn.

"Dude, don't be lame. C'mon."

"Alright. Ask."

"Do you and Chloe have...like phone sex and stuff?"

Ashton flushed. She casually untied and retied the elastic in her long, deep brunette hair until it was back in a messy bun save for a few long, loose curls.

"Oh my god!" Katlyn sat up straighter, giggling. "You totally have!" She grabbed Ashton's arm. "What's it like?"

"Kat, please don't."

"Why? I wanna know. Besides, this is the sorta thing best friends discuss." Katlyn smirked. "So, fess up, lady, is it hot?"

"Aargh." Ashton shook her head. "Haven't you ever...with Matt or something?"

"Phstt. No. We have actual sex. And I really think Matt would suck at phone sex. He lacks...um...the imagination it requires. And honestly, I don't want to hear him trying to figure out how to tell me where he's putting what and shit. Blech."

Ashton cringed. "Say no more."

"Well? How is it?"

"I'm going to exercise my right to the Fifth Amendment and opt out of answering your question."

"Ah! It's hot, isn't it?" Katlyn smirked, nodding enthusiastically.

Ashton rolled her eyes. "I miss her." She exhaled. "Being able to for real kiss her and...yeah."

"I know you do, buddy. But she's planning a visit, right?"

"Yeah. She's been working a lot of double shifts at The Bean and she thinks she might have enough money for a plane ticket by October."

"See? October's a stone's throw away."

Ashton stared blankly at her best friend. "It's two months from now."

"I realize that but as previously stated it's my due diligence as your BFF to be optimistic and supportive lest you forget."

"I didn't forget and I appreciate your efforts but it doesn't make the missing disappear." Ashton cleared her throat before it could fully choke up. "But neither does talking about it. So tell me, how are you and Matt?"

"That's sweet of you to ask but you know there's nothing new to report."

"Indulge me. I'm begging you."

Katlyn squinted thoughtfully. "Okay. Welp, I got him to listen to *a* song by Eliza Diamonds and he actually tolerated it. Like I might have even witnessed a little head bobbing to the beat."

Ashton laughed. "Nice." Her eyes brightened. "That reminds me. Chloe said the concert was awesome. She emailed me some pictures but I haven't uploaded them. I'll send them to you once I do."

"Cool beans. I'm glad she had fun, but I still think it blows that you didn't get to go."

"Me too, but Chloe did mention that Noah didn't complain at all and supposedly he even clapped after every song. He's come a long way."

"Awe. The men in our lives are growing up so fast." Katlyn chuckled.

"Some of them at least, not all."

"Are we talking about your father now?"

Ashton motioned to a few papers on her desk. "He's written me a couple of letters since I refuse to take his calls. He keeps saying he loves me and he loves Chloe and accepts us and that he's sorry blah-buh-dee-da. It's exhausting reading the same apology over and over again."

"What are you going to do about it?"

Ashton flopped backwards onto the mattress. "Chloe and Mom say that holding grudges creates bad energy or whatever."

Katlyn nodded. "Does that mean you're going to write him back?"

"Ughhhh. Most likely."

"I think it'll be good for you."

"Maybe. Maybe not."

"Ash!" Mrs. Daniels hollered from the living room. "Can you come down here?"

"One sec, Ma!" Ashton shouted back. She glanced at Katlyn. "Sorry."

Katlyn waved away Ashton's apology. "No big. I gotta go anywho. Text me later, yes?"

"Yup."

Katlyn got off Ashton's bed and put her palm against her best friend's cheek. "Chin up, buttercup." She offered a kind smile.

Ashton raised an eyebrow at Katlyn. "Bye, Kat."

"Peace out, homes." Katlyn chuckled at herself as she exited Ashton's bedroom.

Ashton rose to her feet and headed for the living room. When she reached her destination, she stopped short, her breath caught in her lungs. She stared ahead at the open front door, where Chloe stood coolly, her blackish eyes drinking in the full length of Ashton for a long moment. Then she smirked.

"Hey there, good looking."

Ashton closed her lax jaw to swallow. "Chloe." Her heart found its rhythm and began to race. "You're here."

"Yeah, well, I was in the neighborhood and figured it would be super rude if I didn't stop by so, here I am. Surprise."

Ashton's eyes bounced between Chloe and the luggage she was toting. "I can't believe you're really here."

Chloe laughed. "I'm really here and it would be the polite thing to invite me in because it's hot as fuck outside."

"Yes! Come in!" Ashton beamed and ran to the doorway. She wrapped her arms tightly around Chloe. "I was worried about you. I hadn't heard from you."

"Flight attendants tend to frown upon using a cell phone while the plane is in the air. You know, regulations and whatnot." Chloe pulled back from Ashton's grip and touched Ashton's face gently with her fingertips. "I missed you."

"I missed you too! You don't even know."

"Why don't you tell me?"

Ashton placed her hands on Chloe's hips and drew her closer. "Can I show you instead?"

"Yes, please," Chloe breathed.

Ashton tilted her head slightly, still smiling faintly as her lips swept across Chloe's. Chloe held onto the back of Ashton's neck, pulling Ashton in even more, deepening the kiss. It wasn't until Ashton became lightheaded due to a lack of oxygen that she slowly moved her mouth away from Chloe's.

"Mmm." Chloe bit her bottom lip. "And I definitely missed that."

Ashton's face immediately reddened. "Same here." She took Chloe by the hand and guided her into the house. Chloe dragged her suitcase along. Once inside, she shrugged the backpack off her shoulders and put it on the floor by the rest of her luggage. She looked Ashton up and down again before stepping closer to Ashton and placing her hands on Ashton's hips. "Do you want to give me a tour of your bedroom?"

Ashton glanced around. "Wait. Wait. Wait. Where's my mom? She let you in, didn't she?"

Chloe smiled. "She sure did and then she wanted me to tell you that she was going to run an errand I think."

Ashton furrowed her brow. "Whoa. Hold up. This was planned?"

"This was planned."

Ashton gasped. "You conspired with my mom?"

"Umm. Actually, I conspired with your mom, your brother, your father, and your best friend."

Ashton's mouth dropped further. "Kat knew about this?!"

"Yup."

"I don't understand. When? How? Why?"

Chloe cupped Ashton's face in her hands. "Now. With careful plotting. And because I'm in love with you."

Tears blurred Ashton's vision, but even in a haze of happiness, Chloe's features were just as devastatingly gorgeous in that moment as they were the first time Ashton ever laid eyes on her. "You are?"

"Ashton, I've been falling for you since I met you and it's never stopped. The falling. So yes, I am. I'm in love with you." Chloe inhaled, steeling herself.

Ashton stared at Chloe. "Are you nervous?"

"Uh huh."

"Why?"

"I've never said that to anyone before. I've never been in love and—"

Ashton pressed her index finger against Chloe's lips. "Shh."

Chloe nodded slowly. "Okay."

"Chloe?"

"Yeah?"

Ashton smiled. "I'm in love with you. Like really really in love with you."

Chloe let out a breath. "Okay good because I'm here to stay...for college at least."

Ashton's eyes widened. "You are?"

"I've yet to declare my major, but Rose University, here I come! All thanks to rolling admissions."

"When did you even apply?"

"Er. The night before you left Boston." Chloe blushed a little. "I told you I wasn't going to let you go; that I want you. So I made it work." She paused to study Ashton. "Is that alright with you? I realize you weren't expecting this."

"It's more than alright." Ashton released a soft laugh of disbelief. "And no, I wasn't expecting you to come here, but truthfully, I wasn't expecting you to come into my life in any way. At all. And yet, you're the greatest unexpected thing that's ever happened to me."

Chloe's mouth turned upwards at the edges and she kissed Ashton. "I'm calling it. You're my home now."

"I'm so down with that because nowhere has felt like home without you."

"In that case, I'll be your home too."

"I'd love that."

Chloe held Ashton close. "Welcome home, Ashton."

Ashton smiled into Chloe's soft, blonde hair, planted a small kiss below Chloe's left ear and whispered, "Welcome home, Chloe."

The End

Printed in Great Britain
by Amazon

64290337R00099